WILD FIRE

Wilder Irish, book seven

MARI CARR

PRAISE FOR WILD FIRE

"It's unbelievable watching each of the men and women **come alive** and **find their love**." ★★★★★ *Kitty Angel, Goodreads*

"This edition of the Wilder Irish Series has a little more suspense than the past stories. I was completely wrong about who the villain was, and **loved every minute of it**." ★★★★★ *Jenna, Goodreads*

"Combining a sweet romance with a great family dynamic, hot flirty banters, and thick sexual tension, you got a **beautifully crafted** story of love in the hot July." ★★★★★ *Carol, Goodreads*

"I loved the Collins family so much and with every book in the series **I love them more and more**." ★★★★★ *Moran, Goodreads*

"Mari Carr **has done it again!**" ★★★★★ *Lynne, Goodreads*

"An excellent romantic suspense, with some sweet Collins shenanigans, and a dominant bodyguard falling for his charge, a former child star turned grown up star, **this book had me engrossed in it from the first page!**" ★ ★ ★ ★ ★ *Dar, Goodreads*

"Mystery and intrigue, love and family lead to a book that had me on the edge of my seat from beginning to end! I **can't get enough of the Collins clan**, and this book just proves why!" ★ ★ ★ ★ ★ *Jennifer, Goodreads*

This book is dedicated to Debby.
For all the miles we've walked, bingo cards we've daubed, stories we've
plotted and bitches we've bitched.
You'll always be my Ouiser!

ACKNOWLEDGMENTS

Every good librarian will tell you the secret to success isn't to *know* all the answers. It's to know *where* to find them.

The answers to my questions as I researched and wrote *Wild Fire* came from many wonderful sources, and I'd like to acknowledge them for the patience they showed as they responded to the three million and twenty-two questions I posed.

Special thanks to Sidney Bristol, Desiree Holt, Bianca D'Arc and Theresa Hissong for filling me in on the details of life on the road with a rock star.

And to Lexi Blake for teaching me about the dead man's switch and how to stop a bomber at twenty paces.

I'd love to add Lila Dubois to this list, but I'm not sure how helpful her advice of "everything is solvable with either a good BDSM scene or C4" really was.

WILD FIRE

He'll risk everything to keep her.

He's going from military hero to bodyguard? Well, that might not be so bad. The money will be good anyway. But then Fergus meets the woman he's hired to protect. A former teen pop star? Please God, no.

After being taken advantage of repeatedly throughout her career, Aubrey Summers is used to pushing people away. But her sexy bodyguard's need for control is eventually impossible to resist. Who is she to fight when he insists on being much closer than arm's length?

And keeping the sexy hero close isn't such a bad idea, considering she's got a stalker.

"Boom! I got you, Pop Pop. Now you have to die."

Patrick Collins placed a hand over his chest and gave what he considered an Oscar-worthy death scene as eight-year-old Fergus giggled.

"You got me," Patrick said, gasping his last. He remained still for about three seconds, then opened his eyes to find Fergus standing over him, holstering his now-empty Nerf gun.

They'd been playing cops and robbers for the last half hour, Fergus always assuming the role of a champion of the law, Patrick relegated to the bad guy.

Once Patrick was back on his feet—hearty and hale again—he and Fergus walked around the living room, picking up the foam bullets.

"Want to play again?" Fergus asked.

Patrick shook his head. "I think this villain needs a cup of tea. How about some milk and chocolate chip cookies? Riley sent them up from the restaurant."

Fergus nodded eagerly, his stomach always winning out over playing. He was a sturdy boy, not unlike his fathers. While Patrick knew that Lily, Killian and Justin were aware of who Fergus's true father was, they'd never told anyone else, insisting

Killian and Justin were both his dad and one sperm wouldn't change that.

Patrick put the kettle on, smiling as he watched Fergus struggle to take the gallon of milk from the refrigerator. He knew better than to offer to help. His young grandson was fiercely independent, probably due to the fact he was an only child and therefore used to entertaining himself.

He was the spit of Justin, but his demeanor was all Killian. In fact, too many times today, Patrick had almost called Fergus by his father's name.

They placed four of the cookies on a plate, then Patrick poured the tea and milk and they returned to the living room.

"Would you like to watch TV?" Patrick offered.

Fergus shook his head. "Can you tell me one of your stories?"

For all his rough-and-tumble ways, he was a quiet lad, the type who preferred to get lost in a book rather than mindlessly watch television. While the Nerf guns and roughhousing came from Justin and Killian, the introspection and keen mind was definitely inherited from his mother, Lily, who was a marine biologist at the Baltimore Aquarium.

Patrick smiled at the request. A fair hand at weaving a tale, there was nothing he loved more than telling a story, and Fergus was one of his biggest fans.

"Well, I think I could be persuaded. Have I ever told you what your name means, Fergus?"

Fergus's eyes widened with excitement. "No. What does it mean?"

"Fergus comes from Fearghas, who was an Ulster King."

Fergus frowned, confused, so Patrick backed up.

"There's this thing called mythology. Old stories. Legends about the people who lived hundreds, nay, thousands of years ago. Ireland has its own mythology."

"Ireland is where you're from."

Patrick nodded. "It is, indeed."

"And I know about mythology. I have a book about it that

Daddy reads to me. About Zeus who can throw lightning bolts from the sky and Hercules, who's super strong."

When Fergus first started talking, Killian had become Dad and Justin was Daddy.

"They were gods about a billion years ago and now they're stars in the sky," Fergus continued. "Dad lets me look at them with his telescope."

Killian had developed an interest in stargazing in the past few years, much to Patrick's delight. He'd been a huge fan of the constellations in his younger years as well, but he had never had the time—or money—to do much more than glance up at the sky to admire them and wonder.

Now that Killian had taken up the hobby, Patrick had begun reading books about the stars and taking his own turn with Killian and his telescope on clear evenings.

"Then you know exactly what I'm talking about," Patrick said. "Zeus and Hercules were gods in Greek mythology. Ireland has different stories. There were four great cycles in Irish mythology, including the Ulster Cycle. During that one, there was a king called Fergus mac Roich, who was known for his strength and virility."

"What's vir—virun—"

"Virility," Patrick said again. "It means manliness."

Fergus liked that definition. "I'm a strong man. Just like my daddies. I'm going to be a soldier like they were."

Patrick knew Fergus's hopes and dreams for the future very well. Just as he knew Lily was praying they never came to pass. She, Justin and Killian had been the best of friends during high school. Then Justin and Killian joined the military, both stationed in the Middle East for a time, and Lily had spent a fair amount of that time worrying.

While Justin and Killian were proud that their son wanted to follow in their footsteps, Lily was struggling with the idea.

Patrick consoled her by mentioning Fergus was only eight, and his dreams were those of a young boy, but that reassurance didn't work. Despite being young, there was a confidence and—Patrick tried to put his finger on the word, then he landed on it—wisdom in Fergus that made everyone, children and adults alike, believe him when he spoke. It was odd to say that about someone so young, but Patrick could only assume that as the only son in a house with three adults, he'd missed out on some of the playfulness of childhood, the sibling squabbles and such, assuming a more mature personality instead.

Of course, what Fergus lacked in siblings, he made up for in cousins and friends. He'd seen Fergus roughhousing with his cousins—he and Finn enjoyed wrestling far too much—and he fit in well with children, laughing, running and talking just as loud as the other youngsters whenever they were all together.

However, unlike Patrick's other grandchildren—with the exception of Ailis—Fergus was able to sit for long periods of time, quietly reading and playing without the need for constant entertainment.

"I think you'd make a fine soldier," Patrick said. "King Fergus was a soldier as well. And his history was a wild one filled with love and adventures, wars and deceit."

For the next half hour or so, Patrick recited the cleaner parts of King Fergus's tale, skipping over the man's renowned sex drive. In true Irish fashion, Patrick took great liberal license with the accuracy of the story, embellishing and adding bits about battles when Fergus asked questions he couldn't answer.

As the story wound down, Fergus leaned his head on Patrick's arm. He was an affectionate, sweet lad. "Do you miss Ireland, Pop Pop?"

Patrick nodded. "Very much, lad."

"I'd like to go there someday. Maybe we can go together."

"There's nothing I'd like more."

"You think I'll win a bunch of battles like King Fergus did when I'm grown up and go to war?"

Patrick nodded. "I'm sure you will. You're a brave lad, strong, honest. But I hope you understand that most battles can be won without force or fighting."

Fergus tilted his head and it was clear he'd never considered that. "How?"

"Through patience and kindness. I suspect every war in history could have been avoided completely if both sides had simply opened their ears and their hearts, listening with wisdom rather than emotion."

With any other grandson, Patrick might have worried about the lesson flying over their heads. Not Fergus.

The young boy listened, then he considered it. "Why don't people do that?"

Patrick shrugged. "I suspect it's because they didn't have wise old Pop Pops telling them to do it."

Fergus giggled.

"Fergus, you'll discover when you're older that the only person you can control is yourself. If you do the right thing, if you offer love and compassion and kindness, that's what you'll receive back. And maybe, others will follow your lead, will try to be good and strong, just like you. Does that make sense?"

Fergus nodded earnestly.

Perhaps it was his old age, driving him to try to push lessons on his young grandchildren. Time was a precious gift. Patrick knew that, had learned it the hard way when his beloved Sunday passed, taken from them far too early.

There was a chance these small lessons would be forgotten.

But maybe, just maybe, they would sink in.

Fergus sat down at his new desk, looked around his sparsely decorated office and grinned. His cousin Finn was across the hall, setting up his own office.

Fergus had been back in Baltimore for seven months, one week and four days. Home after a nine-year stint in the Army, three of those years spent in Afghanistan.

He'd been trained as a military police officer and for a long time, he'd really thought the military was going to be his career.

However, he'd grown tired of Army red tape, following questionable orders and dealing with the worst that civilization had to offer. When it was time to re-up, he'd said no thanks, realizing his presence there wasn't making a difference, nor would it ever. There was simply too much hate in the world, and he preferred to surround himself instead with love. He'd decided it was time to get back to his family and home before he lost all traces of any humanity he had left.

He had amassed a pretty nice nest egg in the service, spending practically nothing he'd earned during that time. And while he hadn't had a clear vision of what he hoped to do upon returning home, one thing was certain. He was ready to be his own boss.

Which was something his fathers could understand. Like him, they'd done their time in the military before coming home to run their own construction firm.

When his dads first heard he was quitting the Army, they'd hoped he would join the family business. Unfortunately, he wielded a gun far better than a hammer, and Fergus liked the idea of being the one giving the orders for once. Joining the construction company would mean trading superior officers for bosses—and dads. His mother had helped him find a way to politely say no thanks to the job offer.

And it wasn't like he was leaving them shorthanded. Uncle Sean had taken a large role in the company, and it appeared his son, Oliver, was destined to follow in his dad's footsteps, a talented carpenter with a genuine love of building things.

Fergus had always felt a particular affinity toward Oliver, probably because, like him, Oliver had been raised an only child by three parents. Well, sort of an only child. Uncle Sean and his spouses, Lauren and Chad, had taken in countless foster children over the years, and Oliver remained in touch with pretty much all of them, claiming them as lifelong siblings even if the placements lasted only a few weeks or months.

Fergus smiled as he thought about his large extended family. He had returned to Baltimore in the middle of his cousin Caitlyn's wedding reception back in September, weary after nearly twenty hours of travel. Ten minutes in the midst of the Collins clan and he'd known he had been right to quit the military.

After the wedding, he'd dumped his duffel in the room he shared with Finn in the Collins Dorm, and he hadn't regretted his decision to return home for one second.

"I'm going to pop across the street for a cup of coffee. Good thinking finding office space near the Daily Grind," Finn said, poking his head in through the open doorway. "Want a cup?"

Fergus pointed to his Yeti thermos. "Nope. I'm good."

"Be right back." Finn was grinning from ear to ear, the big-ass smile a permanent fixture ever since they'd agreed to go into business together. While Fergus had been following orders and traipsing around in the dust and dirt of the Middle East, Finn had been floundering at home.

Growing up, he and Finn had always been tight, probably because they were close in age, Finn just one year younger. Fergus had always wanted a sibling, while Finn—who'd been blessed with two little sisters—had longed for a brother. To meet those needs, they'd grabbed hold of each other—and Finn's best friend, Landon—and somehow, despite their personality differences, they'd grown closer than any brothers ever dreamed of being.

Fergus was just a bit too serious—okay, a lot too serious—but Finn was easygoing with a great sense of humor. Fergus had always been goal-oriented and driven, while Finn preferred to fly by the seat of his pants. And while Fergus had graduated top of his class in high school and taken advantage of all the training and courses he could while in the military, Finn had been a solid C student in high school—something he pointed out had gotten him the same damn diploma as Fergus—swearing he had no aspirations for college.

So, when Fergus returned home in September and found Finn drifting aimlessly from one part-time job to the next, he knew it was time the two of them took control of their futures. Then Finn had shocked the hell out of him by confiding he'd started taking courses in business administration at a local community college. Of course, typical Finn, he didn't have a clue what he intended to do with that degree. He just knew he wasn't cut out for bartending or the military or food service or factory work, and he insisted that he "rocked a tie."

They both realized it was high time they got their shit together and found their chosen paths. Fergus suggested the two of them should build something together, just like his dads had with the construction company.

Their other close friend, Landon, had found his niche with the police department, and had suggested Fergus consider joining the force as well, but trading one law enforcement job for another didn't appeal to him. Despite that, Fergus knew he wanted to do something in security.

A week after Caitlyn's wedding to Lucas, he, Landon and Finn had bellied up to the bar at Pat's Pub with Pop Pop, with the mission of finding their future.

It was Pop Pop who had suggested they start Collins Security. Fergus's knowledge of firearms and law enforcement techniques combined with Finn's people skills and business administration courses made it an obvious answer.

They started researching what licenses were required, searching for office space and, while they'd been able to pool together a bit of money, it hadn't been quite enough. Pop Pop and Fergus's dads had stepped in to "invest," their generosity and belief in them something that still put a lump in Fergus's throat.

"Hey, look who I found in the parking lot."

Fergus glanced up at the sound of Finn's voice, smiling when Hunter Maxwell walked in. Hunter was newly married to their cousin Ailis, the couple having eloped over Valentine's Day.

"Hunter," Fergus said as he stood to shake the other man's hand. "I didn't know you and Ailis were back in Baltimore. Thought you were still on the road."

Hunter had hit it big on the music scene after winning the *February Stars* singing competition two years earlier. Fergus couldn't turn on the radio these days without hearing one of Hunter's songs.

"We aren't. Back, I mean. Not really. We're performing in D.C. tomorrow night, so we thought we'd sneak away for a few hours to say hi to everyone. Last show of this tour is in Baltimore on the Fourth of July, so we'll have longer to visit then."

Hunter glanced around the office. "Wanted to check out Baltimore's latest security company."

Finn pointed to one of the three chairs in the office, claiming another for himself. "We still have a lot to set up and figure out, but it's getting there. You're actually our first visitor."

Hunter surprised them when he said, "I think I'd like to be your first client."

Fergus wasn't sure what to make of that request. Hunter had a first-rate security team. He knew that for a fact because he'd shadowed Hunter's security supervisor one day earlier this year, asking countless questions about his role. He and Finn had researched as they'd tried to determine what type of services they wanted to provide. In the end, they'd decided to make their initial focus private investigation—something Fergus had done a great deal of in the military—and event security, perhaps offering things like personal and IT security as the business grew.

"Client?" Finn asked.

"Not for me, actually, but for a," Hunter hesitated briefly, "friend."

Something about his tone belied the *friend* descriptor.

"What sort of security does your friend need?"

Hunter leaned back. "A bodyguard."

Fergus started to shake his head. Right now, he and Finn were a company of two, looking to hire and train employees. They were nowhere near ready to provide someone with a bodyguard.

"We're not really equipped to do that. I mean, we're still in the building phase. I don't have anyone employed who could—"

"No. You misunderstand. I'd need *you* to be the bodyguard."

He laughed. "It's day *one*, Hunter. We're not even out of the starting gate. I can't leave Finn to—"

"It's a short-term gig. Only six weeks. And you wouldn't just be a bodyguard. There's some investigation required as well. I heard Pop Pop tell Ailis that was your specialty."

"Hunter," Fergus started again, determined his answer had to be no. It was too soon for him to drop everything for a job like this; his first priority had to be getting the firm rolling. "Maybe if you were coming to us in a few months—"

Hunter wasn't deterred. "You and I both know the best way to get business for a company like this is word of mouth. Trust me, if you take this job and do well, you'll have set Collins Security up for success. Plus, it's good money. Like, *good* money."

Hunter had clearly been coached by Ailis because damn if he didn't know all the right things to say. The short time frame, the promotion for the company, and the chance to perhaps pay back some of the money his family had invested were all extremely tempting.

There had to be a catch.

"Who would I be guarding?"

Hunter swallowed heavily, and Fergus realized the other shoe was about to drop.

"Aubrey Summers."

Finn was out of his chair, nearly sending the piece of furniture backwards to the floor. He caught it deftly with one hand as he said, "We'll take the job. *I'll* be her bodyguard."

Hunter rolled his eyes. "Jesus, Finn."

"Who the hell is Aubrey Summers?" Fergus asked.

Finn's eyes nearly popped out of their sockets. "Are you fucking kidding me right now? Aubrey Summers, as in *Sweet Flames* Jenny Sweet?"

"Am I supposed to know who or what that is?" Fergus felt like he was at least six steps behind on this conversation all of a sudden.

Finn threw his arms up dramatically. "You really needed sisters, man. You have some serious holes in your pop culture knowledge. Aubrey Summers played Jenny Sweet on the Family Network's *Sweet Flames*. Sunnie and Darcy were crazy about it. Never missed an episode. Every now and then we'll watch the repeats for a lark and sing the songs. It was an awesome show."

Hunter grinned at Finn's enthusiasm. "I didn't have any sisters, Fergus, and *I* watched the show. It was about a teen pop star trying to find a normal boyfriend while living a very rich, screwed-up sitcom life. Her band in the show was called Sweet Flames, and she ended every show with a new song."

"Why would *you* watch that?" Fergus asked Hunter. "I can see *him* being forced to sit through it with sisters, but you're an only kid."

Hunter grinned. "I liked the music. Aubrey wrote all the songs she and Sweet Flames performed on the show, and they were good. She had four albums go platinum before she was nineteen. Got her start when she was just three in commercials, then the *Sweet Flames* gig came along when she was thirteen. She played Jenny until she was nearly twenty, touring whenever the show was on hiatus. She is a seriously incredible songwriter."

"I take it she's not still on that show?" Fergus wasn't sure how Hunter knew Aubrey, and why he was hiring a bodyguard for her.

Finn shook his head, sighing in a way that told Fergus he still hadn't caught up. "No. The show's been off the air six years. What the hell do you think repeats are?"

Fergus leaned back in his chair. "Fine. Got it."

Finn continued. "She disappeared for a little while, then reappeared with a new solo album a year or so ago. It did really well, didn't it?" Finn looked to Hunter to fill in the details of Aubrey Summers since she stopped being a part of Sweet Flames.

"Yep," Hunter said. "Her comeback album was off-the-charts amazing. Her star is on the rise again. She had some trouble after the TV show was canceled, bad press, bad luck, bad people in her life."

"I think I remember reading about that. Didn't her mom screw her over or something?" Finn asked.

Hunter nodded. "Yeah. Her mother, Candace Summers, had been her manager her whole life and basically stole all of Aubrey's earnings from *Sweet Flames* and the record sales. Said she was saving and investing for her daughter. Instead, she was taking extravagant trips, buying designer everything and, if the rumors are right, financing several lovers as well."

"Wow. Who robs from their own kid?" Fergus mused.

"Aubrey is on tour with me right now because we share a record label. According to Ailis, Aubrey requested to join the tour herself, which shocked me. She's a way bigger name than me. She replaced Jules Shaw after she fell during a big number and broke her leg and arm a couple of months ago. Adding Aubrey saved the tour. Hell, it took it to the next level. We're sharing the headline, and every show since she was announced as the replacement has sold out. We've even added extra concerts. All of them sold out as well."

Hunter was doing a huge cross-country tour. Fergus recalled meeting Jules just briefly when he'd shadowed the security supervisor back in early March. A few nights after his visit, there'd been a mishap with some faulty lift equipment onstage and Jules had taken a nasty fall. The news said she'd been nearly a story and a half above the stage when the rigging failed.

"Man," Finn said, clearly still suffering from some leftover teenage hormones in regards to Aubrey Summers. "You gotta let me do this, Hunter."

Hunter didn't reply. Instead, he looked at Fergus for help.

"Finn, you're the office manager, remember?" Fergus said. And while Finn said he was okay with that, he *had* asked Fergus to teach him about guns and police procedures. The two of them —plus Landon, and Landon's partner on the force, Miguel—had a standing Wednesday-night routine where they'd gather in the Collins Dorm, push back all the living room furniture and go through a training session together.

It hadn't taken more than three Wednesdays for them to decide Finn was probably safest behind a desk.

"You've been to the shooting range with me less than a dozen times and we're only a third of the way through the lessons on restraints."

"But, Fergus—"

"Besides," Fergus continued, "you're clearly infatuated with her. It's bad form to drool while on guard duty."

Hunter laughed.

Fergus leaned forward. The dots weren't connecting. "I'm

still not sure why *you're* here. Doesn't she have her own people who should be doing this?"

"It's not Aubrey who's hiring you. Like I said, she and I have the same record label. I dropped your name to a couple of the bigwigs during a meeting last week. They're concerned about a... situation. Something they're trying to keep out of the tabloids, something they'd like you to investigate while guarding her. It's, um..."

Hunter kept pausing, stalling.

"Just say it, Hunter. What's going on with this woman?"

"She's still in the middle of a sticky lawsuit with her mother over all the money the woman stole when she was her manager. It's been dragging on for years. Then she caught her fiancé in bed with her mother this past Christmas. There was also this nasty scene a couple of weeks ago, where she punched her bodyguard. He's suing for assault and battery, while she's claiming he sexually assaulted her first. People are questioning her story because she was extremely intoxicated at the time, and she's sort of famous for her temper. She's broken a lot of shit."

Fergus took a moment to digest all that.

Before he could speak, Finn sat back down. "Yeah, I think you should be the bodyguard, Fergus. I'll keep things rolling here."

Hunter chuckled, but Fergus didn't find much to laugh about. Their company needed the money and experience. Working as a bodyguard for Aubrey Summers would certainly be a great resume builder for them.

"Who am I investigating? The former bodyguard or the mother?"

Hunter shook his head. "No. I actually haven't gotten to the bad part yet."

"All of that *wasn't* the bad part?" Finn asked dramatically, his eyebrows nearly touching his hairline. "Jesus H."

"Finn." Fergus raised his hand to quiet his cousin down. Sometimes he was grateful for Finn's ability to express his emotions so freely. He called things as he saw them, and Fergus was a big fan of knowing exactly where he stood. At other times —like now—his outbursts made it hard for Fergus to maintain his objectivity and reason things out. "What needs to be investigated?"

"This is the part the record producers want to keep under wraps. We think that Aubrey has acquired a stalker."

"You think?" Fergus asked. "That seems like something you would know one way or the other."

"There have been a couple incidents. A couple of weeks after Aubrey joined the tour, we were playing a show in St. Louis. Chaifetz Arena. One of the security guards on an upper level was badly injured during the last song when someone rolled an M80 at him. The noise of the concert—the music, as well as the crowd screaming—was deafening, so only the people in that section heard the thing go off, and even a lot of *them* weren't sure what it was. The guard was stationed near an exit, so it was easy to extract him without too many people realizing anything had even happened."

Finn blew out a loud breath. "How bad was he hurt?"

"The thing exploded right under him, catching his pants on fire. He suffered some pretty serious second- and third-degree burns."

"And no one saw who threw it?" Fergus asked.

Hunter shook his head.

"That hardly proves Aubrey has a stalker."

"I know. Except that same security guard made some big display of kissing her hand just before the show, and later he was loudly boasting to the crew as well as fans that he and Aubrey always hooked up after the concerts."

"Still nothing," Fergus said.

"*Then*, a rose was tossed on the stage right after her show. Not uncommon. There are always more than a few flowers...but one of the others had a note attached to them. One of the stage-hands always gathers the flowers and arranges them in bouquets for Aubrey. She found the note. It said, 'He'll never touch you again.'"

Fergus leaned back and considered that. "What else?"

"We were in Palm Springs for a show a couple of weeks ago. That's where the incident with the bodyguard went down. After the argument between he and Aubrey, the cops were called in, they took both their statements, and the bodyguard was relieved of duty. The event organizers arranged to have a rental car delivered to the theater so the bodyguard could drive himself to the airport. It caught fire just a few miles away from the concert venue. The bodyguard managed to pull over and get out, but it was a close call."

"Could have been faulty wiring."

"According to the rental place, it was a brand-new car. Police investigated the fire and said the vehicle had been tampered with."

"Let me guess...there was another rose," Fergus added.

Hunter nodded. "This rose was left outside the door of her tour bus that same night."

"Isn't that guarded?"

"The lot where it was parked is, but not the actual bus. No one was inside and it was locked up tight as a drum. No one saw anyone approach it."

"No cameras on the lot?"

"Only one that pointed to that area. It was disabled."

"What did the note on the second rose say?"

"Same. 'He'll never touch you again.'"

Fergus leaned his elbow on the desk, jotting down the words from both notes. "Sounds like someone on the crew rather than a crazed fan," he mused.

Hunter had obviously considered that. "Yeah. That's what we're thinking too, but this is a big show, like sixty-plus crew members—lighting technicians, sound guys, security detail, stage managers and hands, pyrotechnicians. Plus two bands—mine and

Aubrey's—makeup artists, truck and bus drivers, merchandise vendors."

"Only those two incidents?" Fergus wasn't sure that was enough to prove there was a stalker.

"Aubrey was the one who found the rose after the bodyguard incident. She disregarded it until she heard about the car fire. She came to me and Ailis the next morning with the note...along with *three* others that had been attached to roses delivered to her over the course of her two months on the tour."

"Did they all say the same thing?"

Hunter shook his head. "No. All the other notes said, 'We'll be together soon,' but they were in the same handwriting."

"What does Aubrey say? Does she have any suspects?"

Hunter grimaced. "Honestly, I'm not sure. She was a bit freaked out—and hungover—the morning she brought us the notes. I told her we should call the cops, but she started backpedaling big-time. By the time she left my bus, she'd convinced herself both events were accidents and the notes meant nothing."

"That's kinda weird. She has to know something sketchy and potentially dangerous is going on."

Hunter's expression was somewhat resigned. "You have to know Aubrey. The woman is...well, she's hard to get close to. And then there's her ex."

Fergus sighed. There were too many suspects and not enough evidence. "What about him?"

"He keeps popping up at random shows, begging to talk to Aubrey. Apparently, he regrets cheating with her mother and wants Aubrey back."

"Was he in St. Louis and Palm Springs?"

Hunter nodded. "Yeah, but he's shown up for at least half a dozen other shows as well, where nothing has happened."

"Was he there when the other notes appeared?"

"Aubrey wasn't sure, and she says the handwriting on the notes isn't the ex's."

Fergus considered everything Hunter had told him. "Who's her current bodyguard?"

Hunter glanced at Finn, then back at him. "I realize I'm probably not selling this very well."

"Hunter," Fergus prodded.

"She's been through eight since firing the one she hit. Fires them almost daily. She's imploding—drinking too much, screaming at everyone. That's why the CEO of Villatore Records, Isaac Villatore, doesn't want word of this to get out. Her popularity stems from the TV show, so the label is projecting that image of her. She's supposed to be Jenny Sweet, the girl next door, not some wine-guzzling, angry, abusive diva."

"You're right," Fergus said. "You're not selling this well."

Hunter shrugged. "For what it's worth, I don't think she's as bad as people say."

"Is that hunch based on residual teenage hormones?" Fergus joked.

"No. There's something about her. Don't get me wrong. The woman is seriously prickly." Hunter shrugged. "Aubrey is more than capable of eviscerating anyone who pisses her off, but part of me feels like the bitch routine is just an act."

"Maybe. Maybe not. It sounds like she has plenty to be angry about. So, what's to keep her from firing *me*?" Fergus wasn't about to disrupt setting up the business for a bratty pop star, especially if she was going to toss him out on his ear five minutes after he got there.

"I told you. She's not hiring you. The label is. They're the only ones who can fire you—and they won't."

"What did you tell them about me?" Fergus couldn't understand why a multimillion-dollar record label would come to a fresh-out-of-the-gate security company from Baltimore. There were bigger-name security businesses out there who could handle something like this.

"I told them the truth. That you're ex-military, no-nonsense and a top-notch investigator. Said you were conscientious and discreet. Ailis and Pop Pop have bragged about all your military honors for years, so I threw those in the mix. I wouldn't throw you to the wolves if I didn't think you could handle it."

"In other words, none of the legit companies will take the job."

He sighed. "Several of them have. Those are the bodyguards she's fired. Word is out on her now. No one will touch this job with a ten-foot pole."

"Great," Fergus muttered.

Hunter gave him a sympathetic shrug. "If it helps, Aubrey and Ailis have forged a bit of a friendship...if you can call it that. I think it actually falls along the lines of Aubrey tolerating Ailis, but you know that cousin of yours. She goes through life believing there's nothing a Collins can't fix, and she's made Aubrey a project."

Fergus chuckled. "She gets that from Pop Pop."

Hunter gave him a rueful grin. "I've been around both of them long enough that I believe it too. My gut tells me the girl who wrote all those incredible songs when she was Jenny Sweet is still in there somewhere."

"Yeah," Finn said, chiming in after a long silence. "Not going to lie. I wanted to be best friends with iCarly, make out with Hannah Montana, but my dream was to marry Jenny Sweet."

"Are you sure it was your sisters who made you watch those shows?" Fergus teased.

Finn laughed.

"So, what do you think?" Hunter asked after a few quiet moments.

Fergus slid a notepad and pen across his brand-spanking-new desk. "Write down the bottom line. How much are they willing to pay?"

Hunter jotted down the number and slid it back.

Fergus's brow rose, his reaction prompting Finn to rise and look.

"Holy shit, man," his cousin mumbled.

"They're going to pay me *that* much money to protect a pop star for six weeks and find a stalker?" Fergus felt the need to clarify the conditions. Although there was no way he was refusing. It was an inordinate amount of money. More than he'd expected them to make in their first entire year as a business. He could pay his dads and Pop Pop back earlier than he'd expected.

"That's actually just for bodyguard service. Your number-one objective is to keep Aubrey safe. There will be a finder's fee on top of that if you discover who's stalking her, but...well...the producers are more concerned about their star making it to all the sold-out concerts intact rather than catching some crazy super-fan who may or may not have tossed an illegal firework and tampered with a rental car. So?"

"So, I guess I'm going home and packing a bag. Looks like I'm heading back to D.C. with you."

$$\text{❧} \quad 2 \quad \text{❧}$$

"I don't give a shit *what* he's saying. He's a fucking liar, and I'm not giving him one penny!"

Aubrey's lawyer started to speak again, but if she had to hear his condescending voice for one more second, she was going to reach through the phone and strangle the man.

"Goddammit, Ross, stop trying to feed me all that legalese bullshit. I've told you my final answer. I'm not cutting a deal with the prick."

The door to her bus opened, and her latest personal assistant, Blair, walked in with someone behind her.

Great.

Aubrey shot her an impatient look, hoping Blair would get the point, would understand it wasn't a good time to talk, before looking away. She didn't even bother to look at the other person.

Aubrey's focus returned to her computer as she looked again at the ridiculous settlement her lawyer had emailed her this morning.

There was something wrong with a world where a woman was inappropriately groped by an asshole, then had to pay for punching the dickhead's lights out.

"Ross. I'm going to say this one more time, very, veeeery slowly, since you aren't getting it. I'm *not* signing this settlement. I'm taking the asshole to court and you're going to work overtime between now and then to make certain Jesse Richards gets fuck-all for his harassment. He slid his hand up my shirt and grabbed my tit. If anyone should be paying someone off here, it's *him*. Do you understand that, or do I need to find a lawyer who has a pair of balls?"

Ross's response was terse. "I understand."

Finally.

"Good." Aubrey ended the call without a word of goodbye. She began typing, responding to her lawyer's email by restating everything they'd just discussed over the phone. She had learned the hard way, a long time ago, to never leave anything as a verbal agreement. Everything needed to be put in writing.

Blair said her name, but Aubrey didn't bother to look over.

"This isn't a good time," she said, wishing—just once—that Blair would figure out how to read her body language. Why couldn't she tell Aubrey was stressed out and busy?

"I, um, I can see that...but this is important."

"No, it isn't." Aubrey was ninety-nine percent certain that was the truth. Blair rarely showed up to discuss something that wasn't stupid or trivial that she could handle on her own. It was time to admit the new PA wasn't working out and let her go, but Aubrey didn't have the time to hire and train someone new.

Blair was quiet for a moment before shocking Aubrey by forging on. "Your new bodyguard is here. I wanted to introduce you."

Just the word *bodyguard* sent Aubrey's blood pressure into orbit. She continued typing up her email. "Told you. Not important. Give him the drill. Tell the Rottweiler where to stand and make sure he knows to stay the hell out of my way. If he can manage that, he might last longer than the last three guys."

Aubrey was aware the other person on the bus was the bodyguard, and he could hear her rude comments, but she didn't spare the man a glance. Why bother? Now that she knew who he was, there was no point. She went through bodyguards like panties. This faceless moron wouldn't be here next week.

She expected to hear the door to the bus close behind them.

What she *didn't* anticipate was the bodyguard moving around Blair, his outstretched hand appearing in her peripheral view.

"Ms. Summers. I'm Fergus Collins."

Aubrey was a singer, extremely aware of pitch and tone and sound.

Fergus Collins spoke with a beautiful, deep, rich timbre that woke up parts of her that Aubrey had assumed died a painful death.

Unable to resist, she looked up.

Then she rolled her eyes. "Jesus," she groaned, not bothering to hide her outright annoyance. "Seriously, Blair," Aubrey said, even though she was looking at Fergus. "Did Marcus run out of legitimate options?"

"What?" Blair asked stupidly.

Aubrey didn't have the time or energy to waste on the woman, so she decided to take care of this business herself. She'd thrust the responsibility of finding a new bodyguard on the tour manager, Marcus Webber, but he was an idiot if he thought she'd go for this.

Fergus's hand dropped when it became obvious she wasn't going to shake it.

"Listen," she said, hoping Fergus wasn't as thick as her assistant. "I don't know if you're an aspiring model, actor, singer or what, but trust me, you're not going to get discovered by posing as my bodyguard. So why don't I save us both a lot of time right out of the gate? This isn't going to work."

She turned back to her computer. Simply because she didn't think it would help her make her point if she started drooling on the gorgeous man.

Fergus Collins was next-level hot. She'd been surrounded by sexy men her entire life, so the fact that this guy turned her head, proved as much. His dark brown hair was just a touch too long in a way that made her want to run her fingers through it. He had piercing chocolate-brown eyes framed by perfectly shaped brows, and a five o'clock shadow that drew her attention directly to his full, very kissable lips.

And his face wasn't even the best part of the package. It came in second to his broad, muscular shoulders and chest. He wasn't like the usual juggernaut-type guys either, wearing his T-shirts too tight in an attempt to show off all his muscles. Instead, Fergus was sporting a light blue button-down that fit him just right.

"I'm not an aspiring anything," Fergus said, not backing down. "As your assistant said, I'm your new bodyguard."

She glanced over impatiently. She really, truly didn't have time for this song and dance. Her head was aching from the bottle and a half of wine she'd drunk last night...alone.

"You don't honestly expect me to believe that, do you?"

Fergus stuck out his hand again. "I'm Fergus Collins, from Collins Security. And yes, I do expect you to believe that because it's the truth."

Aubrey looked at his hand for a few seconds, then lifted hers, accepting the handshake. She wasn't sure when she'd lost the ability to perform common niceties, but somewhere along the line, she'd become suspicious of everyone and everything, including a damn handshake.

How pathetic was that?

Fergus's hand was large and calloused and strong. Strangely, it was those facts that convinced her that he really *was* who he said.

"You're too pretty to be a bodyguard." She hadn't meant to say that aloud, but exhaustion was kicking in—and it was only ten in the morning. She wished even more she hadn't made the inane comment when Fergus smiled, revealing perfect white teeth and—fuck her—dimples.

Her heart skipped a beat...actually, several. The man was too stunning to be real. There had to be a catch.

"It's nice to meet you, Aubrey."

No. Hell no.

The sound of her name on his lips had her pressing her legs together, trying to still the twitchiness in her very lonely pussy. She needed to dig deep and find the strength to put this whole thing on the right track.

"Ms. Summers," she corrected, adopting the bitchy tone she'd perfected in the last six months. Most days, she didn't even recognize her own voice, but it didn't matter. Life was a lot easier when people were afraid of you. A lifetime of being a doormat had proven that.

Fergus's eyes narrowed for just a second, long enough for her to know she'd achieved her goal.

He didn't like her.

Good.

"Here's how this is going to play out," she continued. "You'll ride in one of the other buses with the crew. When we're at the venues, you'll have two stations. When I'm on the bus, you'll stand outside the door like a good little guard dog. You'll speak to no one. When I'm out and about, I expect you to remain behind me, out of sight. There needs to be at least ten feet between us at all times. I don't want a shadow, Mr. Collins. I want the invisible man. Your number-one goal is to blend in with the background. Out of sight, out of mind."

Fergus remained quiet throughout her recitation of his duties, his expression emotionless.

Rather than give him a chance to respond, she decided it was time to dismiss him and move on. The sooner he was out of her bus, the sooner she could take a couple of Advil and a nap.

"Now, if that's all, you—"

"Are you finished?" Fergus asked.

She crossed her arms. "Excuse me?"

"Are you finished?"

Aubrey nodded, taken aback by the question. Most people were desperate to get away from her at this point in any conversation.

"Good. Nothing you said is accurate. I've already stowed my bag up front. I'll be riding next to the driver in the jump seat of *this* bus." He emphasized the word *this*.

"I don't—" she started, but Fergus raised his hand to cut her off.

"You said you were finished," he reminded her.

Aubrey opened her mouth, intent on blasting him for his outright impertinence, but he spoke again.

"Actually, one thing you said was correct. When you're on the bus, I will be right outside that door. But no one is coming in here who hasn't been cleared by me. As for when you're *not* in here, I'm going to be much more than a shadow. I'm going to be stuck to you like glue. Super glue."

She shook her head, but Fergus didn't acknowledge her refusal.

"Whether you choose to acknowledge it or not, you've attracted the attention of someone dangerous, someone who is willing to harm *others* to gain your attention, to impress you. Until that person is caught, I will be the first person you see every morning and the last one you see at night. It's my job to keep you safe. And I'll do that the way *I* see fit. That may not be the way you prefer, but that's how it's going to be."

"No. It isn't." Realizing Fergus was made of sterner stuff, Aubrey turned her attention to the dog she *could* kick. "Blair, please escort Mr. Collins out." She glanced in his direction, feigning a casualness she didn't feel. Aubrey had basically been on her own since she was born, fighting for survival in a cutthroat world. She was a meal ticket to those around her, nothing more.

And no one—not her mother, ex-fiancé or countless body-guards—had ever made her feel safe.

For some reason, Fergus, who was dripping with confidence and strength, did. Which wasn't as comforting as it should be. "Goodbye, Mr. Collins."

"I, um, well..." Blair stammered.

Aubrey closed her eyes and started counting to ten. As much as her weak-assed assistant bothered her, this version of Blair was better than the one who cried every time Aubrey lost her temper.

Before she hit three, Fergus spoke again, drawing her attention back to him.

"I'm not going anywhere, *Ms. Summers*," he drawled, using the name she'd told him to. Somehow, he managed to make that sound even sexier than "Aubrey." Maybe she should tell him to call her ma'am. There was no way he could make that hot. Could he?

"That's where you're wrong, Rottweiler. You're fired. Get off my bus."

Perhaps she could get rid of him with insults. Nothing else was working, and she was getting desperate.

Fergus didn't move. "You can't fire me. You didn't hire me."

She frowned. "What?"

"I was hired by Villatore Records. I answer to Isaac."

Isaac was the owner of her record label. She wasn't sure when the issue of hiring and firing her bodyguards had fallen to the record company. They certainly hadn't hired the past...hmmm, Aubrey had lost count of how many bodyguards she'd had since the Jesse incident. All she knew was that Marcus had hired them on her behalf.

"Fine. Give me two minutes." She picked up her cell, hit contacts and called Isaac. "I just love jumping through all these hoops," she muttered darkly, making certain Fergus picked up on her sarcasm. "I *really* have time for this bullshit."

"Villatore Records, Isaac Villatore's office." Isaac's secretary answered the phone.

"Julissa. This is Aubrey. I need to speak to Isaac."

"One moment, please."

The secretary's cheerful tone vanished the second Aubrey introduced herself.

"Aubrey," Isaac said, when he picked up the phone.

"Isaac. I understand you hired me a bodyguard. I prefer to choose my own."

"That hasn't been working out."

"Neither is Mr. Collins," she said.

Isaac sighed. Loudly. "He just got there, Aubrey. His references are impeccable. He's ex-military and familiar with the music business."

"How?" Aubrey asked. She'd never heard of him.

"He's Sky Mitchell and Teagan Collins's nephew. Hunter Maxwell is now his cousin by marriage."

"So, what you're saying is, I have nepotism to thank for this." Aubrey looked at Fergus as she said that, letting him know she'd figured out how he got his job.

"Not at all, Aubrey. Fergus Collins has been hired for the next six weeks as your bodyguard, just through the tenure of the tour, and I have no intention of firing the man. In addition to taking care of you, we've asked him to investigate the accidents and those flowers you've been receiving."

"Those accidents were just that. Accidents. And the notes are meaningless, unconnected. Probably someone's idea of a joke."

Aubrey didn't believe that at all. But acknowledging that there was some freak out there hurting people because of *her* was terrifying. The only way to combat the fear attached to that was to shove it all aside.

Deny. Deny. Deny.

Aubrey wasn't proud of her coping techniques, but without them, she'd never get out of bed in the morning.

"Fergus is staying. Can you please, just this once, try to get along?" Isaac asked.

Aubrey's temper piqued. There was no way the record producer would give Hunter Maxwell the same patronizing pat on the head or talk to *him* like some petulant child, if he expressed a concern. She was sick and fucking tired of the men in this business never taking her seriously, acting as if she needed everything mansplained to her. "Listen, Isaac—"

"Sorry, Aubrey. I'm late for a meeting. I really need to go. I'll speak to you soon."

Before she could say another word, Isaac disconnected the call.

"Fucking asshole," she murmured as she put the phone back on her desk.

"Are we good?" Fergus asked with a smug smile that would have made her want to smack anyone else. Sadly, coming from him, it simply drew attention to his lips once more.

"I have work to do." She needed a nap. "Go play Rottweiler somewhere else."

Fergus appeared to have adapted to her award-winning personality already. He didn't blink an eye at her insult. "Very well. I'll be right outside if you need anything."

"I need peace and quiet," she muttered.

"I'll see that you're not disturbed then."

There was something about Fergus that made her certain he'd succeed at that. God knew no one else ever did. Blair couldn't make a decision on her own if her life depended on it, Marcus was king of the ass-kissers, constantly hovering and offering fake praise, and her previous bodyguards had been more brawn than brains.

She nodded once, simply because she was too tired to come up with something else bitchy to say.

Blair and Fergus left, and she walked to the bathroom cabinet, rifling through it for the Advil. Rubbing her forehead, she looked at her face in the mirror.

The reflection looking back proved the outside matched the inside. Yesterday's mascara was today's smoky eye, but she wasn't pulling it off. Her hair was piled on top of her head with a scrunchie in a messy, guess-I-should-have-combed-out-the-hair-spray way. She was wearing an oversized, faded T-shirt that said May Contain Wine—that was accurate, as well—and yoga pants.

She looked like shit. Which was fine because she felt like shit too.

Aubrey popped two Advil, then walked back to her living room, trying to decide if she should nap here on the soft leather couch or in the bedroom.

The tour bus was top-of-the-line, luxurious opulence. Glancing around, she acknowledged that the record label had spared no expense, setting her up to travel in grand style.

The bus boasted a large lounge area with long couches on each side, a small kitchenette that held a mini-fridge, coffeepot and microwave. There was a pretty decent bathroom and a lovely bedroom in the back with a comfortable king-size bed.

The driver of her bus, Joel, was an older gentleman who'd spent the past twenty years driving rock stars all around the country. As such, at least he knew the drill and respected her desire for zero conversation. She wasn't here to make friends.

The bus wasn't as large as the ones carrying the crew or bands, or even Hunter and Ailis's. In truth, it felt more like an RV, the space between her living area and the driver and passenger seats open rather than blocked off by a half wall or door. The jump seat Fergus had just claimed spun around so that it could actually be an extra chair in the lounge.

She tried not to think about how close he'd be at all times.

Peering through the bus window, she could see Fergus was true to his word, standing at his post.

She was about to head back to her bed when she spotted Ailis Maxwell racing toward the bus. Fergus grinned, his arms outstretched, and she ran straight into his embrace. He gave her a big hug that looked amazing, along with an affectionate, brotherly—or in this case, cousinly—kiss on the top of her head.

Aubrey tried to recall if she'd ever been hugged like that. She didn't try to remember for long. She knew the answer. She hadn't.

Her mother wasn't the maternal type, and her father was a deadbeat who'd kicked her pregnant mom out before she was even born. Of course, according to her mother, the fucker had tried to come back into Aubrey's life the second she became famous, but Mom shut that down quick, getting a restraining order against him.

Not because she gave two shits about Aubrey's feelings or desire for a father, but because she wasn't about to share the cash cow.

Aubrey had never seen her father. She didn't even know his name. After breaking ties with her mom, she considered hiring a private detective to track him down. But even after her mother's track record for telling lies had been revealed, Aubrey was too afraid to try. Mom claimed the "sperm donor" was a complete loser and Aubrey was lucky she'd never had to deal with him. The fact he apparently hadn't shown up until she was rich seemed to prove that was true.

Aubrey already had one shitty parent, stealing everything she could get her hands on. She didn't want to risk adding another.

Ailis and Fergus continued to talk. While she couldn't hear them, Aubrey could just imagine what they were saying. No doubt Fergus was telling his cousin what a nightmare Aubrey was, and Ailis was probably commiserating. Part of her hoped Ailis would find something—even just one thing—positive to say about her.

Not that they were friends, exactly.

The best Aubrey could say was she'd managed to be distantly friendly with Hunter and Ailis. Primarily because they didn't need anything from her. Lately, all her relationships fell into one category—work colleagues. Whether it was her producers at the label, manager, PA, fellow headliner or the crew members, everyone was held at the same arm's length, and no one was considered a friend.

Aubrey walked to her laptop, intent on closing the lid.

A new email popped up, and she groaned.

"Fuck," she whispered to herself.

It was from Doug, her ex-fiancé. The stupid asshole emailed her daily, something he'd moved to when it had become apparent she'd blocked his number in her phone.

The subject heading "I love you" told her this missive was going to be more of the same. He'd been groveling ever since she'd walked into their apartment—returning home a day early from an out-of-town show—and found him naked with his face between her mother's legs.

They had dated for nearly three years, and she'd seriously thought it was love. He was the one who'd encouraged her to start writing music again. They'd been blissfully, idyllically happy —or so she'd thought. Right up until the second Doug proved to her that what she'd thought was love was nothing more than easy companionship.

She'd been a lonely child—something perpetuated by her mom, who'd been extremely overprotective of her golden goose —and that feeling of isolation had only increased after *Sweet Flames* ended. That was when she'd discovered she was nearly broke.

Enter Doug Wright, a sweet, struggling musician. He'd found her at her lowest point, picked her up, dusted her off, and then... shown her that love didn't exist.

The world was made up of takers and givers. She'd given her trust to the wrong people too many times, and every single one of them had trampled it to dust.

That would never, *ever* happen again.

She deleted Doug's email without reading it, slammed down the lid on the laptop, and walked back to her bedroom.

With any luck, she might actually manage a couple uninterrupted hours of sleep, though she wasn't holding out much hope.

Insomnia was a bitch.

Then she considered Fergus standing guard by the door as she closed her eyes, and that same weird feeling of security washed over her.

For right now, I'm safe.

That was her last cognizant thought as she drifted off to sleep.

$\maltese$ 3 $\maltese$

Fergus stood backstage, watching Aubrey perform. He'd been her guard dog—he was going to have to find a way to break her bad habit of calling him Rottweiler—for one week. During that time, she'd ignored him, saying less than fifty words, the majority of those being stay, sit, and fetch. Which really did perpetuate his feeling of being an overpaid mutt.

Rather than speak to him in a civil manner, Aubrey preferred to shoot him either impatient or annoyed looks, answering his questions with one word or head gestures, and she'd never engaged him in conversation.

He recalled Pop Pop's advice when he'd talked to him his second night on the job. Pop Pop insisted a person caught more flies with honey than vinegar, so while Aubrey bombarded him with rudeness, he responded with polite smiles and easy conversation.

The more Aubrey maintained her chilly, cold demeanor, the harder Fergus tried to break through it. Pop Pop had taught him all about battles, those fought in the middle of a war, as well as the more personal, one-on-one kind, where words were brandished instead of weapons.

So, while she took pleasure in ignoring him and treating him like a guard dog, he'd gone the "kill her with kindness" route.

She was silent, but Fergus was not.

He talked to her constantly, sharing stories of growing up with his cousins, details about his job with the military police and funny anecdotes about things he'd seen that day. So far, Aubrey was proving to be a tough nut to crack, never laughing or even smiling, never asking questions or joining the conversation. Instead, she'd sniff indignantly or pretend to ignore him.

The one thing she hadn't told him to do was stop.

Which told him she was listening.

Hunter had warned him that Aubrey would work overtime to make his life a living hell. Her distrust of bodyguards ranked up there with mothers and fiancés, according to Ailis. She'd told him that as a way of encouraging him to be patient, and for the most part, it worked. Aubrey had been mistreated by those she should have been able to count on.

He got it.

Most of the time.

Then she'd shoot him a nasty look, call him Rottweiler, and he'd have to fight hard to remember why he shouldn't take the bad-tempered little diva over his knee.

He considered the money he was being paid and wondered if it was enough. He was running out of steam one week in, trailing behind a sullen rock star all day, then trying to manage a few hours of restless sleep.

The record label wanted her protected above all else, so he'd had precious little time to investigate the accidents or the notes. Since he'd taken over the job as her bodyguard, there had been no more roses delivered and no more sightings of her ex at concerts. Part of him wondered if his presence alone had been enough to scare the stalker away, or if Aubrey had been right, and the unfortunate events had been accidents and the appearance of the notes a mere coincidence.

He hadn't managed a full night's sleep yet. Sleeping sitting up was a painful endeavor, made even more difficult by the fact Aubrey suffered from insomnia.

Between trying to find a comfortable position in the jump seat and listening to her strum and hum and fight her way through lyrics on the couch in the lounge area in the wee hours of the night, he was lucky to grab more than a couple hours rest at a time.

He tried to make up for that lack of sleep on the nights they stayed in hotels. He always got a room directly across from Aubrey's suite, but he wasn't completely at ease with that arrangement. He worried about not being able to hear her if someone attempted to break into her room, so he spent most of those nights, while comfortably sprawled out on a bed, resting fitfully and fully dressed, as he listened to every sound in the hallway.

Several times, the bus driver, Joel, had encouraged him to sack out on one of the couches whenever Aubrey ventured back to her bedroom, but Fergus recalled her comment on the phone the first day they'd met, about Jesse Richards molesting her. She'd clearly been hurt by the previous bodyguard, and he thought it best to keep a professional distance, not infringing on her personal space.

Aubrey began singing another song, one that had become his favorite in the past week. Like Hunter, Fergus couldn't reconcile the angry woman spitting venom at anyone who crossed her path with the songwriter who'd created so many haunting, beautiful tunes and penned such deep, meaningful lyrics.

Everything he knew about Aubrey thus far were the things others had told him, which meant he couldn't be sure any of it was the truth. He'd heard about the bodyguard incident from no less than six crew members, each one offering similar accounts. No one had seen the bodyguard grab her, but they'd all seen the punch, and they all agreed Aubrey had been wasted.

He'd also gotten four or five different versions of gossip based on the night Aubrey had walked in and found her fiancé in bed with her mom. Interestingly, Aubrey was the one who'd been jilted and betrayed, yet she somehow came out of that story the villain as well, the storytellers claiming the so-called charming ex constantly sent her bouquets of flowers and chocolates, and showed up at concerts proclaiming his undying love for Aubrey to anyone who'd listen.

According to Blair, Doug contacted Aubrey daily, begging for forgiveness, but the "coldhearted woman" wouldn't even talk to him. And the last person to discuss the affair, one of the event planners here in Charlotte, North Carolina, commented that Doug could hardly be blamed for looking somewhere else, given Aubrey's bitchiness.

The more people trash-talked her, the more Fergus felt sorry for her.

Aubrey glanced his way in the midst of her slow song, and he swallowed heavily, even though she narrowed her eyes at him.

Aubrey Summers was two different people, a raging bitch offstage—Hunter hadn't lied about her temper tantrums—and a pure beauty under the spotlights.

Aubrey's appearance had already taken him down hard the first day they'd met. She was the most gorgeous woman he'd ever lain eyes on, and he now understood Finn's and Hunter's infatuation. Glancing toward the crowd, he saw as many men as women present, and there was no denying they were all under Aubrey's spell. She had long, wavy dark hair, big blue eyes framed by thick lashes, porcelain skin and full red lips.

But more than that, there was her music.

Fergus had fallen in love with the songs she sang night after night. Her music was filled with emotion, speaking to him in ways he couldn't even begin to comprehend. Her songs made him feel as if she saw straight to the depths of his soul and understood everything, even the things he didn't get about himself.

And then there was the sound of her voice. In mythological

times, she would have been a siren—and he, the sailor, definitely would have willingly crashed on her rocks.

"She's amazing, isn't she?" Ailis said, stepping up next to him.

Fergus nodded. There was no point in denying the truth, even if Aubrey went out of her way to drive him crazy offstage. Every night since his first on the job, she'd tried to lose him, exiting the stage on the wrong side, darting around crew members to conceal herself, and finding ways to escape him. He'd begun to hate any room that had two doors. It kept him on his toes, and while there was enough Collins in him that he got a kick out of the challenge, there was the larger, military-trained part that panicked whenever she wasn't in sight. Her safety was paramount to him, and she wasn't taking it seriously.

While there'd been no more roses, that didn't mean the stalker still wasn't there, watching and waiting.

"I love having you on the road with us, Fergus. I missed your ugly mug all those years you were away with the Army."

Fergus chuckled, wrapping his arm around her shoulder and tucking her close. Ailis and her sister, Fiona, had grown up on tour buses like the ones they were rambling around the country in right now. Despite the fact he hadn't spent as much time with Ailis as his other cousins growing up, he'd always felt like she was a kindred spirit.

She shared his love of reading, and while the rest of their relatives tended to be loud and boisterous, always ready for the next party, the two of them found pleasure in the quiet times.

"I missed you too."

Dave, one of the three pyrotechnicians on the crew, approached, his assistant, Erick Rogerson, trailing behind him. Fergus had "befriended" both men earlier in the week, trying to get a feel for them. Given the fact both the "accidents" had involved some sort of fire, the pyrotechnicians seemed like the best people to start his investigation with.

Dave, like Finn, had started crushing on Aubrey when she was Jenny Sweet, and "super-fan" was the only way to describe him. He flirted with Aubrey whenever she was around, playfully begging her to marry him.

Erick, in contrast, was a shy guy who blushed and stammered whenever anyone spoke to him.

"Make way for the flames. My future wife is depending on me."

Ailis and Fergus backed up as Dave took his place by the controls. Fergus was always equal parts impressed and terrified whenever they performed this special effect during the show.

The song, her oldest and most famous one, was the last of her set and a showstopper. The fire that erupted as she hit the last high note was a nod to the fact this was the Sweet Flames' signature song. It never failed to drive the fans wild.

Fergus held his breath. They'd done a run-through of the effect this afternoon, like always, but one of the cannons hadn't fired. Aubrey had given Dave an earful for screwing up, and Fergus had felt bad, watching as the affable guy apologized over and over.

As Aubrey hit the final note, Dave fired the cannons, flames shooting twenty-five feet into the air. There were seven in total, each one firing off in tandem until the last and biggest cannon—the one that had failed earlier—erupted with a bang.

Fergus was so focused on the stage, the cannon, and Aubrey, he didn't notice the first few sparks that flickered backstage.

Someone screamed nearby, and Dave reared back as if jolted. That was when Fergus realized the man had received a nasty shock. Dave went down hard, jerking violently as the current passed through his body. A high-voltage wire was exposed and sparking on the control board. It appeared one of the controls had been loosened, the wire beneath stripped.

Erick quickly hit the circuit breaker, killing the electricity to the machine. The flames onstage sputtered out, but the crowd didn't appear to notice the malfunction as the song had nearly ended anyway.

"It j-just started sp-sparking," Erick, who had a stutter, said, his eyes wide and scared, his face white as a ghost, his hands trembling. "Is h-he..."

"It'll be okay, Erick," Fergus said, hoping that was true.

Ailis dialed 9-1-1, talking to the dispatcher as Fergus knelt next to Dave. He was unconscious, but he was still breathing. There was a nasty burn on his hand, the smell of scorched flesh surrounding them.

Her set over, Aubrey came offstage. She exited the right way this time, clearly drawn by the crowd standing at the edge.

"What happened?"

Fergus heard the tremor in her voice.

He stood up, studying the control board. "Someone tampered with the equipment. Exposed a live wire. Dave must have touched it."

"Oh my God." Aubrey was still looking at Dave. "Is he...did he..."

"He's still alive, but I'm worried about that burn."

"His hand," Aubrey whispered.

Dave's hand was bright red and severely blistered, some of the skin and flesh burned away.

"Come on, Aubrey." Fergus needed to get her away from here. Someone was definitely targeting people who upset her, and it had to be a member of the crew. Unfortunately, there were countless roadies traveling with them, taking care of seemingly endless tasks involved in putting on the shows. Because Hunter and Aubrey were both considered headliners, and each put on a big production, the crew number was doubled. He'd asked for and received files on everyone—from Aubrey's crew as well as Hunter's—but Fergus hadn't had time to read all the information.

"But—" she started, trying to turn back to Dave.

Fergus wrapped his arm around her waist—the first time he'd touched her since shaking her hand the day they'd met—and propelled her toward her dressing room.

Aubrey was clearly as shaken up as Fergus because she didn't protest the touch. He escorted her to her dressing room, walking in and scanning the area, making sure no one was there and nothing had been tampered with.

"It was because of earlier, wasn't it?"

Aubrey was sitting in the chair at the dressing table, her back turned to him. He could see her face through the reflection in the mirror—and he realized she'd never truly believed the accidents were merely that.

Fergus nodded. "Yeah. I think so."

"It has to be someone on the crew."

"Yes." As he spoke, he noticed the bouquet of flowers sitting on a small table near the entrance. "Were these here earlier?"

Aubrey glanced over her shoulder and nodded. "Yeah. Typically, the concert organizers put flowers in my dressing room."

Fergus touched the bouquet, moving several stems aside. Sure enough, tucked in between the greenery and bright blue hydrangeas was a lone red rose and small piece of paper.

"Shit," he muttered as he pulled it out.

Aubrey stood and crossed the room, taking the note from him. "He'll never touch you again," she whispered.

Fergus studied her face, impressed by her composure. Part of him expected her to be upset, to cry. Apparently, Aubrey Summers was made of stronger stuff.

"How do we stop this?"

Fergus rubbed his eyes wearily. "I have access to all the personnel files, but I haven't had time to read through them. Been chasing *you* all over the place."

She gave him a tired look. "I need a drink." Aubrey was a fan of wine. He'd watched her put away at least a bottle a night, every night, since joining her on the road.

Fergus walked over to the bottle of Chardonnay, chilling in ice, and picked up a corkscrew to open it for her. "I'm going to start digging deeper tomorrow. Is there anyone on the crew that you recognize or knew prior to this tour?"

Aubrey shook her head. "My last tour was over five years ago, and my mother was still running the show back then. I didn't have many dealings with the crew. Besides, these attacks and the notes have only started since I joined this tour."

"That's true. It just seems like this has all escalated fairly quickly. I can't help but wonder if the person doing this knew you from before, when you were touring with the Sweet Flames."

Aubrey shrugged. "I don't recognize anyone. I'm sorry. The only reason I asked to replace Jules was because I needed to get out of L.A."

"Why?"

"My ex was driving me insane, trying to make amends. He kept showing up at all hours, finding excuses to stop by, claiming he'd left something behind at our apartment after he'd moved out. I wanted to put some distance between us. Not that it worked," she muttered.

"You think he could have something to do with this?"

Aubrey shook her head. "Not really. Doug is a burnt-out, surfing guitarist with very little ambition and less intelligence. This is way beyond the capabilities of his three remaining brain cells."

"And you were engaged to this guy?"

Aubrey shocked him by laughing. It was the first time he'd seen her genuinely smile, and the sound of her laughter was as musical as her singing. He'd been a fool, thinking her beautiful before. A smiling Aubrey took his breath away.

"I've started referring to that relationship as my period of low self-esteem."

"There must have been something about him." This was the first time he and Aubrey had engaged in a civil conversation, and he was anxious to learn more. First, he hoped it would help him discover who might be stalking her, and secondly, he liked this version of her. Maybe he could distract her enough to keep the bitch at bay and this pleasant woman here for a while.

"Doug was fun to be with, easygoing, gentle, kind. After a lifetime of living in the fast lane, working twenty-hour days with a slave-driving mother who always wanted more, being with him felt like a vacation. He didn't ask me for anything. Except money for pot."

"The last two times people were attacked, Doug was around. Have you seen him here today?"

She shook her head. "No, but Blair said she saw him this afternoon. Marcus knows to keep Doug far, far away from me, so I can only assume he sent him packing. I hear from Blair and the crew whenever he's around, but I haven't seen him myself since joining the tour."

"I'll ask around. See if anyone has seen him backstage tonight. Unfortunately, the man seems to have won some fans amongst the crew. If one of them is helping him get access to places he shouldn't have…"

Aubrey sighed. "I'm no fan of Doug, but I really don't think it's him. He's as harmless as a newborn puppy."

Fergus had learned with the military police that it was best to work all the angles, rather than focus on just one suspect. While Doug felt like an obvious answer—one he wasn't dismissing as easily as Aubrey—there were still other possibilities. "If it's not Doug, what about your mother? There's a nasty lawsuit going on between the two of you, right? Do you think she's doing this?"

"No." Her response came quickly, without hesitation.

"How can you be so sure?"

"Because if my mom was behind this, all those accidents would have been set up to hurt *me*. Whoever is doing this seems to want to protect me. My mother wouldn't go out of her way to do that."

Fergus couldn't imagine what it must feel like for Aubrey to go through life thinking her mom hated her enough to harm her.

"So, what do the three victims have in common?" Fergus mused aloud. "Maybe the stalker could tell you didn't like them, and he was trying to get rid of them for you."

"No. That can't be it. I really like Dave. He's funny."

"You could have fooled me."

Aubrey took the wineglass he offered, taking a sip of the wine. "I shouldn't have yelled at him like that. It's the flames. They scare the shit out of me, so when it made that loud popping noise instead of firing, I freaked out a little. It was wrong to take it out on him."

"Jenny Sweet of *Sweet Flames* doesn't like fire?" He meant his words as a joke, but it didn't get him a laugh.

She scowled. "I hate flying as well. Hence the bus. Want to make fun of me for that too?"

"I wasn't making fun of you."

She took another sip of wine, a bigger one this time. "Okay."

"So, you liked Dave. But you weren't fond of the first two guys, were you?" Fergus needed more insight into those incidents.

Aubrey rolled her eyes. "Oscar, the security guard, wasn't the first guy to lie about having sex with me, and he won't be the last. The man was harmless. Always trying to catch my attention with cheesy pickup lines. I just blew him off."

"And the previous bodyguard?"

Aubrey narrowed her eyes. "If I were a mean-spirited person, hell-bent on revenge, I would have torched that asshole's car myself. But since I'm not crazy, I'm just countersuing him. *He* assaulted *me*. Not the other way around. He's just like everybody else in the world, trying to make a quick buck off the pop star."

"I don't believe everybody in the world is out to scam you."

She snorted. "Stick around five minutes. You'll figure out how wrong you are."

This entire conversation had been very enlightening. For seven days, he'd forged an impression of Aubrey he was happy to have disproved. She worked overtime to give the appearance of a haughty bitch, but he could see that was because she wanted to make certain everyone around her kept their distance.

Fergus understood her angry, standoffish attitude was self-preservation, and her actions were like those of an injured animal. She hissed in an attempt to keep danger at bay.

He couldn't blame her. She'd been hurt countless times. Fergus wondered, if the shoe were on the other foot, would he behave the same way?

He'd been raised in a huge, loving family, with three parents who would lay down their lives to protect him. It sounded like Aubrey had never felt loved, cherished, safe.

Fergus could hear Pop Pop's voice in his head, urging him to help her. To be her champion, to help her fight her battles.

He was only here for five weeks more, but Fergus vowed that he'd spend them not only keeping her safe, but showing her there were good people in the world, who would genuinely care about her if she would simply crack the door open a bit and let them in.

Apparently, he also carried the same belief that there was nothing a Collins couldn't fix.

Which meant he could recruit Ailis and Hunter, and maybe even the rest of his family to help, when they got to Baltimore for the last big show. They would be there a day or two prior to the concert and then...his job was over.

There was a knock on the door.

"Come—" Aubrey paused when Fergus placed a hand on her arm.

"Who is it?" he called out over her.

"Blair."

Fergus opened the door and let Aubrey's assistant in.

"The rescue squad took Dave to the hospital and the bus driver just arrived from the hotel. The bus is unlocked and ready if you want to go there. The engineers are with the police, examining the control board."

Fergus wanted to talk to them, but his primary job was protecting Aubrey. He'd call Isaac's secretary in the morning to see if he could get a copy of the police report. Isaac had basically given him carte blanche on information, telling his secretary to give him whatever he requested. What he needed right now was more time to study what he had already.

"We still pulling out tonight?" Fergus asked.

Blair nodded. "The crew hopes to have everything packed up and loaded by midnight. We're just not sure how long the police are going to set us back on leaving."

Fergus had been impressed by everyone's adherence to the tight schedule, living by the motto, "early is on time, on time is late."

Blair asked if Aubrey needed anything, then excused herself.

"I'll step outside while you change out of your costume, then escort you to the bus."

"Okay."

Fergus was just about to close the door when Aubrey called out his name—his real name, not Rottweiler.

"Fergus."

He glanced back at her. "Yeah?"

"Thanks."

He smiled and shut the door.

Progress.

❊   4   ❊

Aubrey stood up, did three more laps around the small lounge area on the bus, then plopped back down on the couch. She was coming out of her skin.

It had been a week since the attack on Dave. After seeing his damaged hand, she'd confined herself to quarters, opting to remain on the bus or in her hotel room, only emerging when absolutely necessary—for sound checks, hair and makeup and, of course, the concerts. During those excursions, she painted on the happiest of faces, kind beyond belief to everyone she saw.

So far, the attacks had been perpetrated on people the stalker thought had hurt or angered her. From this point on, no one was hurting her. No one was pissing her off. Period.

Her newly revealed sunny personality wasn't the only thing to change. Fergus had joined her in her self-imposed confinement, leaving his post by the door of the bus and moving into the lounge area with her.

Unlike her, he didn't suffer from boredom. He was tapping away on his laptop, something he'd been doing nearly every waking hour since the last attack.

He was going over the personnel files on the crew members

again. As far as she could tell, he'd done the same thing at least three times already, tugging on threads, compiling lists of suspects, running extended background checks, calling previous references listed.

All that work...and he'd come up with nothing.

"Do you know these men?"

Aubrey stood up and crossed the bus, sitting next to Fergus at the table to look at his computer screen. They'd played this game countless times in the past week, and each time her answer had been the same.

Glancing at the faces of the three men before her, she knew this inquisition was going to end in frustration as well.

She shook her head. "What do these three have in common?"

That was Fergus's investigation practice. He'd come up with a list of commonalities, things that could point them toward the guilty party, then he'd research each one until he had a list of suspects. So far, he had a list of crew members who'd traveled with the Sweet Flames when they were on tour, who'd been members of her fan club at some point in their lives, and those who'd been connected to the TV show somehow.

"These three were all hired between the time you joined the tour and when the first attack occurred."

Her eyebrows lifted. This was an interesting approach. She looked at the faces longer, read the names. "Erick Rogerson, 27; Tom Brookshire, 38; and Burt Cranshaw, 56." According to his notes, Erick was one of the pyrotechnicians who had worked with Dave—she thought he might be the one who stuttered, but wasn't sure—Tom was in charge of the merchandising, and Burt was a truck driver.

"Have you spoken to any of them?" Fergus asked.

She nodded, then shrugged. "Probably?"

He rubbed his forehead wearily. They'd established early on in the week that Aubrey was shit at names and worse at faces. She'd spent her life surrounded by a revolving door of cast and crew members—on the set of *Sweet Flames* and on her concert tours. As such, she'd stopped looking, stopped trying to put names to faces. She'd lived behind a one-way mirror for twenty-six years, everyone on one side, perfectly capable of seeing her, while she was trapped on the other side, staring only at herself.

"I'm sorry," she said, which was how all of these conversations ended.

Then he'd go back to reading the files and she'd...

Dammit. She was running out of things to do. Her nails were filed to perfection, she found it impossible to concentrate on her songwriting, and the bus had been cleaned to within an inch of its life.

She walked to the kitchenette and eyed the unopened bottle of red wine. She'd been making a conscious effort to drink less. She left the bottle untouched and drifted to the couch, dropping down onto her back dramatically. Not that Fergus noticed.

She needed a distraction. There were still two hours to kill before she had to head over to the stage to run through sound checks.

"Truth or dare," she said.

Fergus glanced up, frowning when he realized she was serious. "Aubrey, I really don't—"

"Truth or dare," she persisted, sitting up.

He glanced at the laptop once, then said, "Truth."

"Do you have a girlfriend?" Aubrey's *favorite* way to pass the time lately was to wonder about Fergus Collins. He was a puzzle she couldn't figure out. No matter how hateful, how bitchy she'd been to him, he never lost his cool. More than that, he didn't duck his head and hide whenever she appeared on the scene.

Instead, he talked to her like a civilized, friendly human being, and he actually seemed to believe she was capable of the same thing. Strangely enough, that approach had worked, and they talked all the time now. After sequestering herself away from any real human interaction for six months, she found herself suddenly unable to stop talking...about anything and everything.

With Fergus around, the world felt a lot less lonely.

Fergus shook his head. "No."

He turned back to the laptop, resuming his work.

"When was the last time you dated someone?" she asked.

"I already gave you the truth."

"Yes-and-no questions don't count. Everyone knows that."

Fergus chuckled. "I'm tempted to call my cousin, Finn, to confirm that. He grew up with two sisters and is more up on female things—like *Sweet Flames*, and probably Truth or Dare—than me. I'm pretty sure you're cheating, making up rules."

"Call him," she said nonchalantly, hoping he didn't call her bluff.

Fergus glanced at his cell, sitting next to his computer on the table. He didn't reach for it. "I haven't had a serious girlfriend since high school. And since it was high school, I'm not sure you can even call *that* serious."

"Really?"

"I've been a little bit busy, Aubrey. In the military."

She wasn't sure what to make of that information. Then she realized it was something the two of them actually had in common. Her list of past boyfriends was ridiculously small as well. Doug hadn't been her only lover, but he had been her longest relationship by far. "Your turn."

"Seriously, Aubrey, I need to..." Fergus pointed to his computer again.

She lifted one eyebrow. She was a stubborn woman and she was bored.

He closed his eyes, blew out a long, slow breath, then said, "Truth or dare?"

She grinned. "Dare."

He leaned back in his chair, his arms crossed over his chest in a way that pulled his T-shirt tighter, drawing her attention to just how muscular he was.

"Show me your tattoos."

She hadn't expected that request. "How do you know I have any?"

Fergus wasn't swayed. "I've caught peeks of color on your shoulder. Show me or call the game off."

"Nice try, but I'm not that easily intimidated." Aubrey stood up and stepped next to him. "I have two."

She turned her back to him, stretching the neck of her T-shirt over one shoulder. Apparently, she hadn't uncovered it enough, because Fergus rose and stretched it a bit more, his fingertips stroking her skin. It was a gentle touch, which made its impact shocking.

Her nipples beaded and her pussy clenched.

The more time she spent with Fergus, the harder it was to keep her hormones in check.

"It's beautiful. I like the way the artist has woven music notes into the wings. Why a butterfly?" he asked.

She never knew how to answer that question. The reason the ink appealed to her was too personal, too hard to put into words. With most people, she just gave the standard "they're pretty" response. And because the basic assumption about her was that she was shallow, they took that answer at face value.

Aubrey wondered if he'd react the same way.

"They're pretty," she said.

He narrowed his eyes and shook his head. "Try again."

Damn. Perfect response.

She nearly glanced back to see if the butterfly inked on her shoulder had migrated to her stomach, which started to flutter. "I like butterflies. They're delicate, fragile and...free. They can fly away."

"Do you want to fly away?"

She nodded without thinking. "Always."

He was quiet for a moment, and she wondered if he'd press her for more. It was a relief—and a disappointment—when he asked, "Where's the other?"

She turned to face him, enjoying his brief look of surprise when she unfastened the button of her cut-off jean shorts. She didn't need to lower the zipper. She lifted her shirt a few inches as she pulled the hem of her shorts down an inch or so.

Fergus appeared to like the up-close-and-personal tour of her tats. He dropped back down into his chair, his knees outstretched so that she stood between them. He took over, holding her shirt up and away. "What is it?"

"It's a Celtic design that represents strength." This one, unlike the colorful butterfly, was smaller and simpler, inked only with thin black lines.

"I like it. It suits you."

"I got it after I caught my ex with my mom. I walked out of our apartment and drove straight to the tattoo parlor. Probably not the smartest thing to do. Get a tattoo in the heat of the moment, but I needed…"

"Strength," he finished. "Do you regret getting it?"

Aubrey shook her head. "No. Not at all."

They remained there, quiet for a few moments more, Fergus still looking at the tattoo riding low on her hip. Part of her longed for him to close the distance and kiss it.

Tension—purely sexual—hovered in the air around them. The temperature on the bus suddenly felt unbearable, and her insides quivered.

Fergus had been the definition of professional, a gentleman. Yet there was something about him, something she couldn't put her finger on, that told her he wanted her just as much as she wanted him.

And as certain as she was of that fact, she was just as sure he would never act on that desire. Would never cross that line.

If she were a better person, she wouldn't feel the overwhelming urge to tempt him.

"Truth or dare?" she whispered.

He glanced up at her, then slowly lowered her shirt, shifting away.

"Truth," he chose again.

She snickered lightly. "Coward."

Fergus shook his head. "Wise."

Aubrey returned to the couch, thinking about what she wanted to ask. The main question she wanted an answer to slipped out before she could think better of it. "Since you don't have a serious girlfriend, I'm curious. When was the last time you had sex?"

Fergus, true to character, never blinked twice. "August."

"It's the beginning of June now. That was a long time ago. Who was she?"

"My first response wasn't a yes or no."

She grinned. "But it was a one-word answer. Those always allow for follow-up questions."

Fergus stood, coming to sit next to her on the couch. "Now I *know* you're cheating. But I also know you'll keep asking until you get your response, so in the interest of moving the game along...her name was Jeanne. She and I went through basic training together, which was where we first hooked up. Our military paths diverged from there, but whenever we ran into each other, we got together. We were compatible lovers."

Aubrey crinkled her nose. "Compatible sounds boring," she teased.

Fergus didn't laugh, but she could tell he didn't take offense either. "Compatible in this case means she would let me handcuff her wrists together, bend her over the nearest flat surface, spank her ass and fuck her from behind."

Aubrey sucked in a deep breath, perfectly aware that Fergus heard her gasp.

"Oh," she said. If every inch of her being wasn't focused on the forceful clenching of her pussy, she might have tried for more words. She couldn't spare the energy. Instead, she was wondering if, one, she had time to pay a visit to her vibrator, and two, if she did, would Fergus hear her and—please God—join her in her bedroom?

"In case you haven't noticed, I prefer to be in control—in and out of the bedroom."

She wished she had the strength to smile, but every single thing he said merely turned her on more. She could understand his desire for power. Aubrey had spent too much of her adult life struggling to hold on to control. It was exhausting, but with no one she could trust to rely on, she'd had no choice. The idea of giving Fergus control over her—even if it was just her body in the bedroom—sounded like heaven.

Aubrey swallowed heavily, fighting to shake free of whatever spell he'd cast on her. "I don't need anyone to con—"

He chuckled. "*You* need it most of all."

Their gazes were locked, neither of them denying the truth of what he'd just said. She could scoff, dismiss it as bullshit, but he'd know she was lying.

Then what would he do?

Punish me.

The thought of Fergus punishing her every time she behaved like a brat shook her to the core...and made her long for something she'd never dreamed of.

"Truth or dare," Fergus murmured. It figured he'd get into the game just as she was struggling to recall her own name.

"Truth," she said, before recalling that wasn't what she wanted. "I mean da—"

"No. Rules state you have to stick with your first choice."

She laughed, albeit weakly, when Fergus decided to do a little cheating of his own. "Fine."

"What are your hard limits?"

Aubrey opened her mouth, but no sound came out. Were they talking about having sex? Was he propositioning her, or was this still part of the game?

When the silence stretched too long, Fergus broke it. "Do you understand the question?"

She nodded. "I...can't...think of any." It probably didn't help that her experience with the type of sex play he was discussing was limited to...none.

Suddenly, all she could see was Fergus, binding her to the bed, blindfolding her, spanking her, taking parts of her that had never been touched before.

This was the most sexually charged moment of her life, and Fergus hadn't even kissed her, hadn't touched her except for that soft brushing stroke on her shoulder. God, all he'd done was talk to her, plant seeds, draw pictures. He should be the songwriter, not her.

"Do you want to hear mine?" he asked.

"Yes."

"I don't whip women with anything other than my hand. I don't humiliate them. And I don't share."

She realized her lack of knowledge had impacted her hard limits response. "I don't think I know enough to fully answer your question."

"I'm aware of that."

She didn't like the dismissive tone in his voice. It suggested that he didn't consider her the type of woman he could dominate in the bedroom.

"Truth or dare," she countered before he could end the game and walk away.

"Dare."

"Kiss me."

He shook his head even before she'd finished issuing the dare. "No. The game stops here."

"Why?"

"You know why."

Aubrey didn't want to admit that she did. If they kissed, it wouldn't stop there. It would carry over to her bedroom, where she'd let him test every single one of those hard limits he was curious about. And while her body was screaming out for that, her chest started to grow tight, fear creeping in.

He reached over and cupped her cheek, the sexy, brooding

man she'd been playing the game with vanishing, replaced by safe, friendly Fergus again. "The things I ask of my lovers require absolute trust, Aubrey."

Aubrey hated that fucking word. "I can't...give you...that."

He smiled kindly, and she thought maybe even sadly. "I know."

$\maltese$ 5 $\maltese$

Fergus jerked awake at the sound of a cry. Or was it a scream?

Joel, the bus driver, looked at him. "Sounds like Aubrey's having another one of her nightmares."

She cried out again.

"She has nightmares?" Fergus asked.

Joel nodded. "Hasn't had one of them since you hopped onboard. Was sort of hoping having you close by was helping her. I don't mention them to her anymore because I think it embarrasses her. She's had half a dozen or so since joining the tour. Just a heads-up. She'll be meaner than a wet hen tomorrow."

Fergus stood up.

"What are you doing?" Joel asked.

"Checking on her."

The driver shook his head. "Seriously, man. I don't think she'll thank you for that."

"I'll take my chances."

Joel had obviously taken some serious abuse at Aubrey's hands in the past few months. Enough to steer clear. Fergus didn't blame him for that. During his first week, he'd seen her lash out at countless people, so he understood why so many members of the cast and crew still kept their distance, even though Aubrey was trying to be nicer.

After the attack on Dave, she seemed to realize the best way to keep those around her safe was to practice kindness. It had taken him a few days to recognize that was what she was doing, and then a couple days more before it occurred to him that being nice came more naturally to her than the bitch routine.

He'd also met the ex, Doug, a couple of days ago, and while he hadn't discounted the man as a suspect, he understood why *she* had...and maybe even why she'd considered marrying him. He was exactly what she'd described—a goofy, good-natured, shaggy-haired, hippie-looking...dude.

God knew he'd said that *word* enough to convince Fergus that's what he was.

Fergus had caught him backstage during Aubrey's show and escorted him to an empty dressing room, where he'd interrogated the man. Doug claimed he'd slipped one of the security guards—some *really chill dude* he couldn't name or describe—a twenty to gain entrance.

Doug had been clueless about the accidents—and visibly sad about Dave, whom he'd met and considered a *seriously cool dude*—and had no flowers with him. Doug had jumped at the chance to leave Aubrey a note, clueless Fergus wanted it for a handwriting sample, and not because he was being a *totally awesome dude* for offering to pass the missive along.

Aubrey had been right. The writing samples didn't match. More than that, the poor bastard didn't even know how to spell the word "together," penning "togther" instead.

Even the stalker knew how to spell.

Doug had teared up, asking if Fergus thought he had a chance of winning her back. When Fergus said no, Doug crumpled, shaking his head and blaming himself for being such a *stupid dude*, and swearing the thing with Aubrey's mom had been a one-time thing and the biggest mistake of his life.

Fergus had actually found the guy sort of funny and exactly as Aubrey described—dim-witted, harmless, affable enough.

She cried out again as he walked the length of the bus to reach the door to her bedroom.

Now that he understood her fear of being hurt again was what drove her to push people away, leaving her to fight her demons on her own would only convince her that she really was completely alone in the world.

He knocked quietly on her closed bedroom door. "Aubrey?"

Silence.

He said her name again.

"Go away."

Typical response. Ever since their Truth or Dare game, Aubrey had pulled away from him, determined to resume the distance she'd maintained during his first week as her bodyguard. Mercifully, she hadn't returned to calling him Rottweiler, though he thought he might prefer that to this polite stranger routine they'd fallen into.

"No," he said.

It was quiet again. He considered his next move. He wouldn't walk into her bedroom uninvited. That was the quickest way to take two steps back in this game he was playing to win her trust. Three weeks into the gig and in a lot of ways, it felt like they were still at day one.

Before he'd had too long to think, she said, "Come in."

He opened the door to find her sitting up in bed, wearing a light pink T-shirt with a kitten on it. It was surprisingly playful when compared to her usual take-no-prisoners personality.

"You okay?" he asked from the doorway.

She gestured around the room. "No bad guys."

He hadn't thought there were. He'd done a thorough check of the bus before allowing her to board it.

"Bad dream?"

Joel hadn't lied. Aubrey didn't like admitting to the nightmares.

"I let you in to see I'm fine. Now go away."

Fergus leaned on the doorjamb. "Want to talk about it?"

She narrowed her eyes. "No. I don't."

"I have bad dreams too," he admitted. "Was stationed in the Middle East for a few years with the Army. Saw some things that just won't leave me alone when I close my eyes. Funny how things that seem tolerable in the daytime can haunt you in your sleep."

She studied his face a few moments before nodding. "Yeah. That's true."

Then she surprised him by picking up a notebook and pen from her bedside table, quickly jotting something down.

"Diary?" he joked.

She shook her head and continued writing. "No. Song ideas. Haunted dreams," she murmured, more to herself than to him. She even hummed a few notes that certainly fit the emotion.

"You think and feel in music, don't you? My aunt Teagan is the same. We'll be in the middle of a normal conversation and then boom, she disappears for a few hours to strum her guitar and put lyrics and melody to a feeling."

"You know, I'm a huge Teagan Collins fan," Aubrey admitted. "I bet I've listened to her songs a million times in my life. She inspired me to start writing my own music."

He grinned. "Maybe I'll have a chance to introduce you. She'll be in Baltimore for the final concert on the Fourth of July."

"Ailis told me. I'm excited about that...and also terrified. It's sort of intimidating to sing in front of your idol."

"Don't be scared. Teagan is the sweetest, gentlest soul on the planet. Ailis is a lot like her. She and my uncle Sky are amazing. Talented."

"You never had any musical ambitions?"

Fergus shook his head. "I appreciate music more than I can say. It really drives my mood, either to energize me when I'm working out, or to make me feel better on a down day. But nope, no skills. Can't sing. Can't play a musical instrument. My mom pushed me to do piano lessons, but that didn't last more than a few months. I think my dads were happier than I was when she said I could quit. Figured if I couldn't manage "Skip to My Lou" after six months of lessons it was never going to happen, and they were sick of listening to me fuck it up constantly."

"Dads? I didn't get the sense your parents were divorced. So your mom remarried?"

"No." Fergus had learned from a very young age that there were three types of people in the world: the ones who accepted his parents' unusual lifestyle, the ones who disapproved outright, and then, the worst kind—the ones who pretended to think it was okay, but made jokes about it behind their backs. "My mom is legally married to my dad, Killian. But she's also—not officially —married to my daddy, Justin. They've been in a committed threesome for thirty years."

"You have three parents?"

Fergus nodded, waiting to see which camp Aubrey would fall into.

"Wow. Lucky you. I don't have any."

Her sad words reminded him why he was there. "What was the dream about, Aubrey?"

"Nothing," she said.

He started to ask again, but she shrugged. "Seriously," she continued. "It's always the same dream, and it's always nothing. I'm in a dark room. No, not dark. Pitch-black. I can't see anything, not even my hand in front of my face. I'm roaming around, trying to find a door or window, but there's nothing. No walls. Just endless darkness. I walk around in the dark with my hands out and there's nothing there. I'm trapped in nowhere."

She rubbed her chest and he could see she was getting worked up again.

"I start to panic, running around, my hands out, searching for a way to escape."

He stepped into the room, wanting very much to take her in

his arms, to console her. He crossed to her bed, standing next to her, hesitating.

Fergus wasn't the type to hold himself back, especially not when a woman needed comforting, but Aubrey was a trickier case. Prickly as a cactus and skittish as a newborn colt.

Even her tattoos felt like contradictions. Her need for strength was a direct contrast to her desire to fly away.

She looked up at him. "The first day you were here, you stood outside the bus. Ailis ran to you, and you hugged her."

Fergus hadn't realized she'd been watching. "Yes."

"It looked nice."

That was all he needed to hear.

Fergus sat on the edge of her bed. Before she could pull away, he tugged her toward him, engulfing her in a tight embrace he hoped would bring her comfort.

She was stiff as a board at first, her arms remaining by her sides. It was obvious Aubrey wasn't accustomed to hugs.

"Put your arms around me, Butterfly. I'm not going to hurt you. I promise."

She didn't react immediately, so he just held on.

Eventually, she wrapped her arms around his waist, the tension slowly melting as she rested her cheek against his chest.

"Don't make that promise," she whispered.

"What?"

She didn't repeat her request, but he didn't push her. He knew what she was thinking. In the end, everyone she loved and trusted hurt her. Promise or not.

Fergus wasn't sure how to help her, how he could counteract twenty-six years of loneliness and emotional abuse. He was only here for three more weeks. Time wasn't on his side.

Then he tried to figure out when his mission had changed. Sure, he'd been hired to protect her, to discover the stalker if he could, but his personal goal had morphed into something much larger and harder.

He wanted to save her. Aubrey was a sad, shattered soul, and it ate away at him.

Rather than talk, he continued to hold her. She was quiet for so long, he wondered if she'd fallen asleep in his arms. He moved away slightly to check, sorry to have done so when she scooted away from him.

There were dark circles under her eyes. No wonder. He'd never met anyone who slept less than Aubrey. He'd pulled double shifts in the military, and even those hadn't left him as tired as he'd been these past few weeks, trying to keep up with her.

"You need sleep," he murmured.

She glanced around the room, and he could see she wasn't holding out much hope that would happen.

"What would help, Aubrey? Sleeping pill?"

She shook her head. "No. I've tried them. For some reason, I just get more wired. I usually drink wine, but that only knocks me out for a few hours, and..." She lifted one shoulder.

"And?" he urged.

"Then it wakes me up in the middle of the night and gives me panic attacks."

"Have you always struggled to sleep?"

She nodded. "It's been worse since the holidays, but yeah, I'm not very good at sleep. Not even when I was with Doug. I used to drive him crazy. Unlike me, he could sleep for fourteen hours straight without even rolling over. I was so jealous of that."

"Lay down," Fergus said, standing up to tug the covers over her before perching on the edge of the bed again. "My Pop Pop used to tell me bedtime stories whenever I had a sleepover at his house. He'd draw all these beautiful pictures in my head until I fell asleep, his words morphing into the best dreams I've ever had. I'll tell you one of them."

She frowned, and for a second he thought she might refuse, might tell him to get out. She surprised him when she said, "No one's ever told me a bedtime story."

Fergus scowled. "Aubrey, I seriously hope I never meet your

mother. I consider myself a calm man, and God knows I'd never lift a hand to hurt a woman, but damn if the things I've heard about her don't piss me off enough to think about it."

Aubrey flashed him another smile, something he didn't see enough of from her.

"You've got a pretty smile."

He shouldn't have pointed it out because it faded the second he mentioned it.

Fergus sighed, but let it go. Everything with Aubrey was going to happen in baby steps. "Once upon a time, there was a brawny, handsome Irishman named Patrick."

Pop Pop had regaled him with countless stories over the course of his childhood—myths, Irish folktales, fairy tales, battles between knights and dragons—all of them filled with adventure and magic. And while he'd loved all of them, Fergus's favorite bedtime story was about when Pop Pop met and fell in love with Grandma Sunday.

"Patrick tended bar at Scully's, in a small town called Killarney, all the while dreaming of the day he would come to America."

"Who's Patrick?"

"My Pop Pop," Fergus replied. "I'll take you to meet him when we get to Baltimore for the last show. My family owns a pub there. Pat's Irish Pub. It's the best place on the planet."

"Ailis has mentioned Pat's Pub before, and your Pop Pop. He sounds like a character."

Fergus chuckled. "That's the perfect way to describe him. He'll love you."

Aubrey rolled her eyes. "Doubtful. In case you've failed to notice, I can't even scale up to the part where people merely tolerate me."

"He'll love you," Fergus repeated, piercing her with a look that dared her to contradict him again. "He'll hear you sing and that will be it. And if you'd let me finish my story, you would understand why."

Grandma Sunday had been a singer. Fergus had wished countless times he'd had the chance to meet her—even just once—and hear her sing. Pop Pop insisted that Teagan's voice was as good as her mother's, and there were times the man swore he couldn't tell them apart.

Fergus continued telling the story about Sunday and Patrick meeting at Scully's, about the wealthy man who almost stole her away, about their journey to America and the way they lived happily ever after above the pub with their seven children.

Aubrey asked questions throughout, her eyes getting heavier with each passing minute. He suspected it wouldn't take her much longer to fall asleep.

"What happened to Sunday?" she whispered, fighting to keep her eyes open.

"She died of cancer a long time ago. Before I was born."

Aubrey blinked a few times, and Fergus wondered if she was fighting back tears.

"That's so sad."

"Yeah," Fergus agreed. "Pop Pop always said he'd been blessed to have as many years with her as he did, insisting Heaven simply couldn't make do without one of its most precious angels." Those words had comforted him as a child, but now, like Aubrey, he couldn't brush aside the sadness, the injustice of her life being cut so short.

They were silent for a few minutes more, then he rose slowly. "Go to sleep, Aubrey. I'll be right up front if you—"

"Will you stay here?"

He hadn't expected her quiet request, but there was no way he'd deny her wish. Aubrey, still shaken from the nightmare, was reaching out to him. And he wasn't going to let her down.

"Sure." He stood up, sitting on a plush armchair near the bed. He'd been sleeping sitting up whenever they were on the road, living for the nights when they stayed in hotels and he could recline in a real, honest-to-God, bed.

Aubrey shook her head. "No. Not there." She scooted over.

Then she put two large pillows down the center of the king-size mattress with a small grin.

He chuckled at her down-feather barriers, but exhaustion was winning the day. "Just for a little while," he said, lying on top of the covers. He was fully dressed—jeans, shirt, socks—and she was perfectly covered, buried beneath the thick duvet.

She rolled away from him and he studied her back, the only light on the bus provided by the full moon and the cars passing them on the highway.

They remained still for a long, long time. He thought Aubrey had fallen asleep. Hell, he was tired enough that *he* should have been out in an instant, but he couldn't manage it, couldn't stop thinking about her...about his unexpected feelings for her.

Fergus replayed the list he'd made after their Truth or Dare game, the one he thought would help him maintain the status quo. Shortness of time, professionalism, and her innocence were all in the cons column. So was the fact he lived in Baltimore and she in L.A.

He glanced in her direction when Aubrey rolled over to face him.

"You asleep?" she whispered.

"No."

She pulled away the pillows separating them, dumping them onto the floor behind her, then shifted toward him.

Despite every reason he'd just listed for why this was a bad idea, Fergus reached for her, wrapping his arms around her as she nestled closer.

"During the Truth or Dare game," she started.

It was the first time she'd mentioned it since he'd refused to kiss her. "Yeah?"

"One of your hard limits was that you don't share."

"That's right." He now understood where her thoughts had drifted.

"But your dads..."

"Share my mother," he finished for her. "I'm like them in a

lot of ways, Aubrey. But in others, I'm my own man. Maybe my lack of willingness to share is because I was an only child. All the toys in the house were mine and mine alone."

"I'm an only child too." She paused before adding, "I wouldn't share either." She was giving him her truth, letting him know what one of her hard limits was.

Aubrey rested her head on his shoulder, and he placed a light kiss on top of her head.

"Thank you for the bedtime story," she murmured sleepily.

"You're welcome."

"Fergus. I know you said you wouldn't, but…do you think you could kiss me? Just a good-night one. Nothing more. I don't know why I need—"

He cut off the rest of her words, his lips pressed to hers. He kept the touch chaste, soft, short.

It was exactly what she needed—and the opposite of what he wanted.

Fergus had known one kiss with Aubrey would destroy him, obliterate all the reasons he had for staying away.

He hadn't been wrong.

"Feel better?"

She nodded. "For now," she whispered. "I'm safe."

Her words shook him to the core.

While he was grateful that his presence made her feel that way, he couldn't deny how much the first part of her statement bothered him.

For now.

Aubrey Summers.

She was a virtual stranger.

She was a pain in the ass.

She was broken and scared.

And, as much as it shocked him to admit, she was *his.*

For now.

❧ 6 ☙

"What's our bet for tonight?" Ailis asked.

Fergus considered his options, studying the stage. "I've made sure she's seen me standing stage left. Stage right would be the obvious choice, but she's already figured out I'll anticipate that move."

Aubrey—despite all her other precautions to protect the people around her—refused to stop playing the stage-exit game. Every night, she left the stage from a different direction, leaving him to try to guess where to catch her. Sometimes he outsmarted her, other times he didn't. And while she always managed to find him almost immediately afterwards on the nights she won, it didn't stop him from suffering several moments of outright panic until she was safely by his side.

He and Ailis had started taking bets—a Collins trait no one escaped—on how Aubrey would attempt to ditch him as she left the stage. He knew the game was Ailis's way of keeping him from losing his shit over Aubrey's antics. It had helped the first couple of nights, but his patience was wearing thin. While the stalker had made no attempts to directly approach her, that didn't mean she was safe. That was something he was going to make damn sure she understood after tonight.

"She could always skirt around the drum set and dash out the back," Ailis suggested.

"Yeah. She hasn't tried that yet, but it's definitely possible."

"This is her last song. Time to call it. I've got ten bucks on the drum-set route," Ailis said. "So I'll cover that angle."

"Okay. I'm betting on this side. I'm going to step out of view, make her think I've crossed to the other side and nab her as she leaves."

Ailis whistled appreciatively. "Bold move. I like it."

"If we're both wrong, you'll get to her before me. Keep her in your sights until I get there. And, Ailis…"

"Yeah?"

"This game ends tonight. Tell Hunter that Aubrey won't be at the after-party. It's time she and I have a talk."

"Good luck." Ailis gave him an encouraging smile and wave as she moved around to the rear of the stage. Fergus had enlisted her help keeping an eye on Aubrey, since it was impossible to cover all the angles alone. There were other security guards he could enlist, but right now, no one on the crew had been taken off the suspect list. He wasn't sure he could survive three more weeks like this. He was starting to feel like a dead man walking, moving through most days like a zombie after managing only a few hours' sleep each night.

"S-sorry, F-Fergus. N-need to run the b-board." Erick had taken over Dave's duties, running the control board that activated the flames for Aubrey's final number. Aubrey had insisted the entire effect be taken out of the show after Dave's injury, but she was outvoted by Marcus. The control board was repaired and, Marcus's only concession, constantly monitored by a security guard.

Fergus stepped aside so that Erick could work the controls. Erick's stutter was more pronounced whenever Aubrey was around, and he flushed bright red anytime she glanced his direction. Fergus understood the man's response to her. It was easy to be intimidated by her beauty and talent.

Erick's name appeared on just one of Fergus's countless lists, as one of three crew members who'd joined the tour after Aubrey replaced Jules. Fergus had taken a hard look at him after Dave's accident because Erick had access to the control board.

Regardless of those two facts, Fergus had shifted the man lower on the list of suspects. He and Dave had been the best of friends, constantly together prior to Dave's accident. With Dave still recuperating in the hospital, Erick meandered around like a lost puppy most days.

Erick fired off the cannons with skill, the board functioning perfectly. Aubrey held the final note, the flames lighting the stage so brightly, it almost hurt to look.

Fergus stepped behind a large speaker as her song ended. The screams and applause of the crowd were deafening. Tonight had been one of her best shows yet.

Fergus held his breath, hating that he was playing her game this way. He shouldn't take his eyes off her, not even for one second, but she was forcing his hand.

The more he considered it, the more annoyed he became. Of course, a lack of sleep wasn't helping his state of mind either.

He counted to five, intent on stepping back around the speaker, when Aubrey appeared. She glanced around looking for him, her eyes widening when she spotted him and realized he'd guessed her path.

Rather than admit defeat, she sniffed in true poor-sport fashion, then walked on. There were dark circles under her eyes too, even despite the heavy stage makeup she was wearing.

Neither of them had slept well the past few nights. He'd returned to the jump seat the night after her nightmare and remained there whenever they were on the road. Aubrey was back to avoiding her bedroom, drifting between dozing fitfully on the couch and pacing the bus like a caged animal.

It had been four days since she'd let him hold her, and then, in true Aubrey fashion, she'd retreated again. Treating him once more like a guard dog, a stranger.

She was frustrating, infuriating...beautiful.

It was a bad time to start this conversation. Neither of them was in a great frame of mind, both running out of steam.

Sadly, recognizing that didn't calm his mood.

"No after-party," Fergus said, falling into step next to her.

"What?"

"You're going to your dressing room, changing, then you and I are taking the van back to the hotel and having a long talk."

Aubrey frowned. "Listen, Fergus, you don't get to dictate to me about what I can and cannot do after—"

"Don't bother finishing that sentence."

Fergus opened the door to her dressing room, pushing her inside and following her.

His patience had reached its limit.

"How dare you manhandle me! I'm telling you right now, Fergus—" she started.

"That little game you're playing is over. No more cat and mouse. Understand?" Fergus was proud of how calm and quiet and steady his tone was, considering he was itching to pull Miss Aubrey Summers over his lap. Part of him got the feeling she was playing the brat simply to provoke a response from him.

Problem was, they both knew what that response would be. And as much as Aubrey might want him—physically—she wasn't ready for what he wanted emotionally.

Her eyes narrowed. "Who do you think you are?"

"I'll tell you exactly who I am," Fergus said. "I'm the man who is busting his ass to keep you safe despite your desire to throw yourself in the path of danger."

"You're kidding, right? I play by your rules every second of the day, hiding on that bus or in a hotel room day and night! The only time I don't have you dogging my every step are those two minutes when I leave the stage. That's the only thing I have control of these days, and I'm not giving it up! If you don't like it, tough."

If Fergus were a different sort of man, he might have responded to her taunt a better way.

As it was...

He gripped her waist and spun her toward the door, pushing her back against it.

He wanted to kiss her. Every instinct was driving him to it. Hell, Aubrey wasn't even fighting.

She lifted her face to him, then licked her lips invitingly.

"You're driving me crazy," he murmured.

Aubrey didn't smile, didn't respond to his confession. Her breathing was rapid, her chest rising and falling, drawing his attention to her cleavage, displayed perfectly by her low-cut sequin dress.

"I want to kiss you, Aubrey."

"Do it," she whispered.

He shook his head just once. "I also want to bend you over that makeup table, lift this dress and spank your ass."

"Do it!" she repeated.

Fergus fought for control. He never struggled to keep emotion out of the bedroom, always remaining calm, stoic, precise, completely in charge—of himself *and* his lover. He prided himself on it.

It wouldn't be that way with Aubrey. She was the queen of extremes—one moment, hell on wheels, a bitch to be reckoned with, the next, sweet, fragile, broken.

Fergus cupped her face, forced her gaze to meet his, so she would understand exactly what she was inviting. "If we go there, you're *mine*. Completely."

She blinked but didn't reply. Instead, her eyes dropped to his lips, and hers parted slightly.

Before he could kiss her, there was a knock at the door.

They moved apart slowly, both breathing heavily.

"I..." Aubrey ran her fingers through her hair, her eyes no longer filled with desire. Now they were clouded, confused. She frowned. "That can't..."

"Happen." One word had never hurt so much to speak, but Fergus couldn't deny the truth of it.

There was another knock, this one louder.

Fergus opened the door to find the tour manager, Marcus, standing there.

"Oh, Fergus. When I didn't see you at your post, I got worried." He looked beyond Fergus to Aubrey, clearly confused to find her bodyguard inside the dressing room rather than standing outside the door. "Everything okay in here?"

Fergus nodded as Aubrey stepped next to him.

"Everything's fine," she replied, her voice somewhat shaky.

Fergus couldn't fault her for it. He was feeling off-kilter too. He'd been attracted to countless women in his life, but nothing that came close to what he was fighting here. He wanted her more every day, until it was a need that bordered on desperate.

"Good," Marcus said, glancing down the hallway. "I was afraid perhaps Doug had managed to make his way in here."

Fergus's jaw clenched. "He's here?"

Marcus shrugged. "A couple of roadies said they thought they saw him before the show, backstage. I've got a bunch of guys looking for him, but if he was here, he appears to be gone now."

"How the hell could he get backstage?" Fergus asked. "I read the security guards the riot act after the last time. Threatened to have the whole lot of them fired if he got in again."

"I don't know. They're working in teams, and all of them swear they didn't let him in. They mentioned being afraid of losing their jobs. I honestly think if they knew who'd let him in, they'd rat the guy out. None of them appear to know anything. They did point out there are a couple of locked doors that weren't manned. Maybe he's got someone else on the crew helping him sneak in and out."

Fergus ran his hand through his hair. "We're going to have to add a couple of guys to the security detail at future shows. This is getting old. I told the asshole in no uncertain terms to stay away."

"I thought that worked. He stopped emailing me after the two of you talked. I haven't heard a peep from him since. Is everyone else okay, accounted for?" Aubrey asked.

Fergus knew what prompted her question. Doug had been lurking around at all three shows where someone was injured. Perhaps that would imply guilt without question, but he'd also been at other shows where nothing untoward had occurred.

And while Fergus wasn't the type of investigator who worked entirely on gut instinct, after talking to Doug, his gut told him the "dude" was harmless. He was a drifter and a leech, a male bimbo who seemed sorrier about getting caught and losing his free ride than actually cheating.

"Everyone is fine. The van is here whenever you're ready to head back to the hotel."

"Okay. I'll just change out of my costume and then we can go."

Marcus looked at Fergus, who nodded at Aubrey. "I'll be right outside if you need anything."

He and Marcus took their leave, and Fergus remained stationed at her door. One of the roadies and Erick approached, letting him know they'd searched the entire backstage area, but hadn't found Doug.

"Thanks," he said.

"Is Aubrey a-alright?" Erick asked, flushing as he said her name.

"She's fine," Fergus said, smiling. "I'll tell her you were concerned."

Erick blushed an even darker shade of red, bobbing his head in unspoken thanks before walking away.

The other roadie, Rich, hung back and rolled his eyes. "Poor guy has it bad."

Fergus chuckled. "He's not the only one. I figure half the crew is in love with her."

"And the other half is female," Rich joked.

The two of them shared a laugh, and then Rich returned to his regular duties.

Fergus took the few quiet moments to try to regroup. He thought he'd managed it until Aubrey opened the door, stepping out in her jeans, light blue T-shirt and boots. She'd slid on her standard ball cap and sunglasses—even though it was night—in an attempt to hide her identity.

The second he saw her, he knew his battle to resist her was lost.

He led the way to a back entrance, the van pulled up close to the door, so they could hop on quickly. A couple more guys from the security detail were already in the vehicle. All of them rode to the hotel without speaking.

When they arrived, Fergus escorted her from the van toward the back entrance of the hotel. He was grateful for the nights they spent in hotels, away from the bus. If he never saw another bus after this, it would be too soon.

"Aubrey!" someone yelled, the call followed by loud screams.

Aubrey had some tenacious fans. They'd clearly discovered where she was staying and had planted themselves at the back entrance in hopes of catching sight of her. The other security guards held back the rushing fans as Fergus shielded her, guiding her quickly to the secured entrance.

They used the employees' elevator, taking it straight up to her suite. Once again, he would be staying across the hall. Given the size of the crowd gathered outside, he foresaw another restless night. If he knew the rest of the security detail better, he'd ask another one of the guards to remain outside her door for the night, but until he figured out who her obsessed fan was, he remained a one-man band.

They were nearly to her door when Fergus spotted the rose waiting outside her room, on the floor.

He held his arm out, holding her back.

"Wait a second, Aubrey."

She stopped, frowning as he walked over and picked up the rose. There was a card attached to it.

He slid it out of the envelope, instantly recognizing the handwriting. He'd studied the other notes enough.

We'll be together soon.

Aubrey stuck her hand out. He shook his head, but she persisted. "Let me see it."

Fergus handed it to her, and she closed her eyes wearily after reading it.

"Fuck," she murmured.

Fergus glanced down the hallway and spotted the video camera on the ceiling. It was smashed.

He kept her room key for her. Sliding it out of his pocket, he unlocked the door. However, rather than letting her walk in without him, he led the way, searching each room. No one was supposed to have access to this floor except a handful of people —the tour manager and personal assistants, he and Aubrey, Hunter and Ailis, and members of their security detail.

The fact that the stalker managed to leave the flower right outside her door was alarming—because Fergus couldn't figure out how the man knew which room was hers and how he'd gained access to the floor.

Aubrey remained near the door to the suite, watching as he did his sweep.

"Okay," he said once he was satisfied no one had gained entrance to her room. "It's clear."

She tried to stifle a yawn, the lack of sleep taking its toll.

"Why don't you head into the bedroom, Aubrey? I'm going to go over to my room and grab my things."

She frowned. "Why?"

"Because I'm sleeping on that couch tonight."

Aubrey shook her head. "No. You're not."

Fergus crossed his arms and grinned. "Yes. I am."

If she hadn't been so exhausted, he suspected she would have kicked up one hell of a fuss, but Aubrey looked as wiped out as he felt. "Fergus. About what happened in the dressing room—"

"I'm sleeping on the couch, Aubrey. Nothing more. Go to your room. It'll be okay."

She sighed, then walked past him. For a moment, he thought she looked disappointed. There was a day of reckoning coming for them, but not tonight.

Neither of them had a clear enough head to make any decisions.

She went straight to her bedroom and shut the door. He didn't miss the sound of her locking it behind her.

He grinned. Smart girl.

Fergus walked over to the couch, not bothering to grab his bag. He was too tired. Lying down, it occurred to him as he closed his eyes that tonight could be his first peaceful night in a week. He liked being close to her, knowing she was only a few feet away if he needed to get to her.

Finally, he could protect her...and rest.

Which meant the sleeping arrangements for the rest of this tour were about to change.

And with that happy thought, he slept the sleep of the dead.

$\mathcal{R}$ 7 $\mathcal{R}$

ubrey laughed as Ailis finished telling her about something silly Hunter had done last night after his set. She had escaped the bus shortly after they'd arrived in Houston. She wouldn't have left the bus at all if she hadn't spotted Ailis sitting on a bench just outside the convention center. It was unusual for Ailis to be out and about so early, so Aubrey had stepped out to make sure everything was okay.

She also needed a few minutes of fresh air, somewhere she didn't feel like she was living and breathing nothing but Fergus.

She'd thought they had been inseparable before.

But ever since finding the rose outside her hotel room, Fergus had closed ranks even more, now sleeping on the couches in her hotel suites. He'd moved to one of the long couches in the lounge area of the bus as well, which meant she either stayed in the bedroom or sat on the other couch, watching him sleep, while pretending to work on her songs.

She couldn't turn around twice without bumping into him.

So far, he'd kissed her just once. It had been the most chaste kiss of her life. It had also been the most exciting.

She wanted to do a hell of a lot more with him.

It was all she could think about, dream about, write songs about. She was consumed with thoughts of him.

Fergus wanted to control her, dominate her in the bedroom. That knowledge had fueled her fantasies for weeks, making it impossible for her to concentrate on anything else happening around her. He probably mistook her quietness of late as her pulling away, but the truth was, she was too hot and too fucking bothered.

She didn't have a doubt in her mind Fergus would never hurt her physically. More likely, the man would rock her world. She spent most nights imagining his lips and hands roving all over her body. She could almost feel the tickle of his beard between her legs. He'd come here with a five o'clock shadow, but he'd stopped shaving last week. It had only improved his stunningly good looks.

Fergus had been nothing short of a complete gentleman, but there was some primal part deep inside her that responded to what she knew lurked beneath his skin. Fergus radiated confidence, control, patience. Those attributes made him a good bodyguard...but they'd make him an amazing lover.

The sex would be off the charts. And if that was all that was at stake, she would trust him with her body.

But it was more than that. Her heart was on the line too.

The more she got to know him, the more peeks he offered into his life, his family, his past, the higher the risk of her falling for him.

She'd sworn after Doug she wouldn't go back there, wouldn't give someone control of her heart, her emotions. Every drop of love she'd had left vanished the day she found Doug in bed with her mother.

Fergus Collins was her bodyguard...for only two weeks more.

Nothing long term could come of this, so the devil inside her kept urging her to indulge. After all, how much could happen in just two weeks?

Sadly, she knew the answer to that.

She liked him. And she was deeply, deeply attracted to him.

Then the stronger, more terrifying voice spoke up.

This was more than attraction. She was starting to trust him.

And that was the one thing she couldn't do.

Wouldn't do.

So she shoved the fantasies away.

Ailis glanced toward the road as a vehicle passed, and Aubrey got the sense Fergus's cousin wasn't just outside enjoying the breeze.

"Are you waiting for someone?" Aubrey asked.

"Just the van," Ailis said, though her tone suggested her response wasn't totally the truth.

The second she had spotted Ailis, she'd thrown on some clothes and snuck off the bus, desperate to escape before Fergus woke up and her hormones started doing the talking for her.

Ailis was welcome company, very much like her cousin. She was an entertaining storyteller with an easy humor. Aubrey was jealous of how simple it was for Fergus and Ailis to be themselves, to be so comfortable in their own skins, while Aubrey's scratched like wool on a rash.

"Uh-oh. Someone looks like they woke up on the wrong side of the bed."

Aubrey turned, looking to see who had caught Ailis's eye, even though she had her suspicions.

Sure enough, Fergus was storming across the parking lot, headed to where she and Ailis sat on the bench, soaking up some of the early-morning sun. They were in Houston for the next two days. Typically, after they arrived at a venue, vans would take them to their hotel. In this city, they were staying in the Four Seasons. She could see the hotel from where she was sitting. It was definitely close enough to walk to. Regardless, by some unspoken law, rock stars didn't walk to hotels. Therefore, they were waiting for transportation.

It was Saturday, so the downtown area surrounding the

Toyota Center was quiet. It always amazed Aubrey how huge cities felt like ghost towns on weekends.

"What are you doing, Aubrey?" Fergus didn't bother with hellos. He didn't even acknowledge Ailis, which spoke to his level of stress. He was usually very kind to his cousin. The past few weeks together had left both of them exhausted, well beyond the breaking point. And while she appreciated his need to keep her safe, she was tired of...well, of fucking everything.

"Aubrey," he repeated.

Why did his voice have to be so damn sexy?

She closed her eyes, cast that unhelpful thought aside, then stiffened her spine and threw her head back. She was tired of being a captive. "Hanging out with Ailis. Enjoying the day. Being a normal person."

Fergus sighed. "I didn't say you could never leave the bus. You shouldn't be out here alone. Why didn't you wake me up?"

"I'd hardly say she was alone," Ailis said, waving her hand as if to remind him she was present.

"You know what I mean." Fergus ran his hand through his hair, causing one lock to fall back over his forehead in a very sexy, very bedhead way.

Ailis must have noticed how exhausted Fergus looked as well. "I don't think there's anything wrong with Aubrey letting you get some rest. To be honest, I'm not sure how you manage any sleep at all in the jump seat of that bus."

Fergus glanced away from his cousin, back to Aubrey, neither of them speaking quickly enough. "I, um..."

Ailis smiled. "Unless...you weren't in the jump seat."

"He sleeps on the couch," Aubrey replied. Except for that one incredible night when he'd told her a bedtime story and lay down next to her.

Fergus held his hand out to Aubrey, intent on pulling her up from the bench. "I'd feel a lot better if you two would chat inside the bus."

Aubrey took his hand without thinking about it, then reconsidered, trying to draw it back. He didn't relinquish it. They struggled for a moment.

"Aubrey."

She dug in her heels. "Let go."

He gripped tighter, his eyes narrowing. "No."

"Goddammit! Let go of my hand. We're just talking, Fergus." She didn't mean to lose her temper, but she was wrecked, physically and emotionally.

"And there are plenty of crew members milling around to see. You can't pretend to know what sets this guy off, Aubrey."

"What is that supposed to..." Aubrey's chest tightened, panic setting in. If she'd put Ailis at risk, she would never forgive herself. "I didn't think—"

"That's right. You didn't think."

Fergus's words enraged her. "Listen," she started.

"It's okay, Aubrey." Ailis shot Fergus an impatient look. "I'm not in any danger. She's been sequestered on that bus and in hotel rooms for weeks, Fergus. Even prisoners in solitary confinement get a bit of time outside."

Fergus tightened his grip on her hand, using it to propel Aubrey toward the bus. This time, she didn't fight him. "Dammit, Ailis. I don't care if she spends the next two weeks locked on that bus twenty-four-seven. People are getting hurt, and this guy clearly wants to get to her. Until I can figure out who's doing it, I want the two of you safe."

Ailis, who was always so patient and peaceful, patted Fergus on the arm, trying to calm him down as she walked next to them. Hunter's bus was parked next to Aubrey's. As they walked, Ailis continued to look down the street. She was definitely waiting for something, and Aubrey didn't think it was the van.

"It's okay. And you're right," Ailis said. "I should have suggested we chat on the bus. It's just such a pretty day. A perfect day. I can't tell you how much I've been looking forward to Houston." Ailis threw her arms up, pointing out the blue sky, the brightening sunshine and cool breeze. "So let's start over. I'm going to go wake Hunter up. See you two at breakfast at the hotel?"

Aubrey nodded, curious about Ailis's enthusiasm. She wasn't sure what made Houston so damn special, but it was nice that *someone* was happy.

Fergus waited until his cousin entered the bus she shared with Hunter, then led Aubrey to hers, following her inside.

"Dammit, Aubrey," he exclaimed once they were inside. Joel, the driver, had already disembarked, joining the crew for breakfast before heading to the hotel himself.

She raised her hand to cut him off. "Don't start with me, Fergus." She'd been so hell-bent on escaping the bus, she hadn't considered she might be putting Ailis at risk. She felt bad enough on her own. She didn't need another one of his lectures. "I'm in no mood. Trust me, this won't end well for you."

If someone could have scripted the exact worst thing to say to him in that moment, those probably would have been the words. His brows furrowed, his eyes darkened with anger.

"Not in the—" His voice was a blast of noise in the quiet bus, but he regained control quickly. Very quickly.

Aubrey wondered what it would be like to push him too far, to tempt the beast out of its lair. Impulse overrode common sense. She wanted Fergus, and she knew exactly what to do. He responded to the brat, the haughty diva.

And if that failed, well, at this point, she'd take the fucking fight.

"I'm not your prisoner." She walked away from him toward the refrigerator, eyeballing the half-consumed bottle of white wine, very tempted to pop the cork and take a long swig.

Instead, she pulled out a bottle of water. "If I want to take a walk, I will, and there's not one thing you can do to stop me."

The bottle flew from her fingers when Fergus gripped her arm, spinning her to face him, backing her up against the wall. It was an alpha move that had her body clenching in sweet anticipation.

"You don't want to push me on this, Aubrey."

She sniffed in true bratty-style, dismissing his threat, even as her pussy clenched. "Go back to your post, Rottweiler. You're starting to bore me."

His expression was fierce, his jaw tense. Any woman with half a brain would have relented, but she knew he wouldn't hurt her. At least not in any way she wouldn't love. Her favorite fantasy was the first he'd painted for her.

Fergus binding her hands behind her as he bent her over the table, spanking her. She pressed her legs together trying to still the pulsing, aching need.

It didn't help. She wanted him, unleashed, in charge, taking her in every dark, twisted, kinky way he could come up with.

He studied her face too intently. "I'm giving you one more chance to stop. If you keep acting like this, you're going to find out exactly what happens to bratty little girls who don't do as they're told."

Fuck.

Yes.

She went for the throat and rolled her eyes. "Are we done here?" she asked, pretending to fight a yawn.

Fergus smiled, if she could call it that. A pack of starving wolves probably bared less teeth and looked less dangerous.

His grip on her upper arm tightened as he leaned toward her and gave her the kiss of the century.

Fergus dropped all pretense of restraint, the "perfect gentleman" vanishing into thin air.

He pressed her lips apart, his tongue thrusting deep. He released her arm, opting instead to hold her still by her hair. His fist closed around her ponytail, pulling it until she gasped, her scalp stinging.

His other hand ventured to her neck, his large palm engulfing it from behind, his fingertips resting over her racing pulse.

Everything he did screamed of power and control. If anyone else were touching her this way, she would have been terrified.

With Fergus, she only wanted more.

He kissed her long and deep, Aubrey awash in the sensations. She tried to shift closer, wanting to feel more of him.

The kiss softened, gentled, and that touch was even more potent than the rougher claiming. Aubrey mewled against his lips, savoring this moment. Then the hand holding her hair loosened and he pulled the hairband out, running his fingers through the long tresses, caressing the sting of her scalp away with soothing fingertips. It was a kind gesture, a caring one.

Her chest tightened—and she pushed away.

"Don't," she said, her breath ragged.

Fergus was breathing heavily too, and though it appeared to cost him, he started to step away.

"No," she stopped him. "Don't stop. I just…" Aubrey struggled for a way to explain. "You can't be nice to me, Fergus. My past boyfriends were nice to me, making me think they cared about me, and then…"

He cupped her cheek. "Aubrey."

She shook her head, moved away from his hand. "I need what you said. Just sex—rough, raw, hard. I can't take it if you're nice to me."

He ran his hand through his hair, but he didn't move to resume the kiss. For a moment, she feared she'd gone too far, shown him exactly how fucked-up she was. If he was a smart man—and Fergus was—he'd walk away from her and never look back.

Then he surprised her. "Open your legs."

She complied, and he shoved his knee between them, pressing it firmly against her center. She responded like a bitch in heat, dry humping it in the hopes of finding some sort of relief as he resumed the harder, powerful kiss.

This. This was what she needed.

Sheer primal possession. To be taken.

It had to be that way. Aubrey simply didn't have it in her to offer anything freely anymore. He would have to claim and take.

"More. You. Want you," she murmured against his lips. She wanted to strip off her clothes and his, wanted him to drag her to the bedroom, tie her to the headboard and fuck her so hard her bones shook.

Fergus pulled away, shaking his head. "No. Bad girls don't get rewards. They get punished."

"Yes," she whispered. God. He got it. He understood.

Fergus groaned as he kissed her again, hard and quick. "God-dammit, Aubrey."

"Don't," she whispered. "Don't stop. Don't think."

He kissed her again, but once more, it was gentler, and though he held her upper arms, his grip loosened. She couldn't let this end here, couldn't let him pull away because he thought it was the right thing to do. So what if it was?

She was tired, scared and lonely. She'd like to say that was something new, but in truth, she'd felt that way for as long as she could remember.

With Fergus, all those things faded. They would be on tour for two more weeks. Just fourteen days.

Aubrey intended to take advantage of that time.

He stepped back, and she started to complain. Her words dried up when he reached to cup her breasts, squeezing them in his large, rough hands.

She barely had time to enjoy that touch before he moved again. This time, he pulled her forward, toward the table, bending her over it, then following her down.

He kissed the side of her neck briefly before biting her earlobe. "Last chance, Aubrey Summers. Once I pull these jeans off, I'm going to punish you for putting yourself and Ailis at risk this morning, then I'm going to fuck you...going to make you mine."

"Yours," she whispered, wanting to try it on for size. Nothing had ever sounded more incredible. Even if it was only for a short time.

Fergus moved upright, his hand striking her denim-covered

ass twice. He wasn't holding back. He was showing her exactly what she was asking for, giving her one last chance to walk away.

She couldn't.

She wiggled her ass, inviting him to spank her again.

Fergus had just reached around her waist to unfasten the button on her jeans when there was a knock at the door.

Both of them stilled, neither speaking.

"No," she whispered.

Fergus didn't move. Like her, he was probably hoping whoever was there would just go away.

Another knock.

The blinds were pulled, so they couldn't see who was outside. Mercifully, whoever was outside couldn't see them either.

When the person knocked a third time, Aubrey realized they weren't going away. Fergus stepped back and, just like that, the most exciting moment of her life faded to nothing.

She pushed herself upright on shaky legs. Her insides felt like mush, her wits completely gone. Fergus offered her a steadying hand. Like her, he appeared slightly rattled. His jaw clenched tightly.

Aubrey was terrified that her one chance with him had passed. That Fergus would regroup and that would be the end of it. Two more weeks of sexual frustration and distance and loneliness.

She blinked rapidly several times, trying not to cry.

"This isn't over," Fergus said, his voice deep, sure.

She struggled to catch her breath. "Promise me."

He pulled her toward him, his hand gripping the back of her head. "This isn't over," he repeated, stronger than before. "You're *mine*, Aubrey." Then he sealed the proclamation with a hard kiss.

One that ended when a fourth, louder knock sounded. "We know you're in there! Ailis told us you were."

Aubrey didn't recognize the male voice, but it was clear Fergus did when his eyes widened with obvious delight. "Holy shit!"

He strode to the door, unlocking and throwing it open. "Finn!"

Aubrey watched as Fergus's cousin and partner in the security company strode onto the bus, followed by two more men.

"Landon! Miguel!" Fergus hugged each man, clearly thrilled by their arrival.

Aubrey wished she'd thought to duck back to her bedroom. God only knew what she looked like at the moment. Her hair was probably a mess, her lips felt puffy from Fergus's rough kiss and one glance downward proved her nipples were budded, evident through her T-shirt and bra. She had no idea how Fergus had managed to recover so quickly, but her body was still raring to go.

She forced a smile when Fergus's cousin Finn glanced her way. She recognized his look instantly. Unlike Fergus, Finn had clearly been a fan. She was used to men—close to her age— looking at her with lingering teenage love in their gazes. Finn wasn't looking at her like she was Aubrey—he was seeing Jenny Sweet.

It wasn't until that moment she realized that was another part of Fergus's appeal. He looked at her and saw...*her*. The real her.

Or, well...the horrible, bitchy, fucked-up version of her. She should probably consider seeing a therapist once the tour was over.

Finn smiled shyly, but it was the man Fergus had called Miguel who spoke first.

He approached her, kneeling in dramatic fashion. "I'm here, my darling. The love you've been searching for your whole life. There's no need to look any further. Prince Alexander is here."

Fergus crossed his arms and scowled while Finn rolled his eyes. The other man, Landon, snickered.

Aubrey recognized the line. It was from one of the episodes of *Sweet Flames*, which had been filled to the brim with ridiculously over-the-top, cheesy dialogue like that, all of it followed by the canned laugh track meant to make viewers think it was funny rather than stupid.

Sometimes when she looked back on those years, it felt as if she'd been having an out-of-body experience throughout the entire filming of the series. It was the only way she could explain being able to say her lines without gagging.

Regardless of the origin of the line, she couldn't help but get a kick out of Miguel's introduction. Especially when he gave her a very charming grin and a wink that let her know he thought the lines were just as outrageous as she did.

"Are you sure that's the role you want to assume?" she asked. "Jenny dumped the prince in the end, you know."

Miguel rose slowly, shaking his head. "Damn. I knew there were going to be long-term effects from missing the last season of the show. My mom lost her job and we couldn't afford cable. Never saw *Sweet Flames* after that grand gesture on the prince's part. Who did Jenny end up with?"

Aubrey laughed. "Josh."

Miguel crinkled his nose in feigned disgust. "The housekeeper's son? Her best friend? That boy was boring, no flair for romance or the dramatic. Hell, he wasn't even hot."

Aubrey nodded. "I told the writers the same thing, but they were determined."

"Seriously, Miguel. Get a grip, man." Finn stepped closer. "Hi, Aubrey. I'm Finn. I'm sure Fergus has told you all about me. About my charm and wit, my natural athleticism and sheer brute strength." He backed up that pronouncement by flexing for her. "I guess you can see, now that I'm here, I got all the looks in the family. Poor plain Fergus just got the book smarts."

Aubrey glanced from Finn to Miguel and back again. She wasn't used to being around such funny, unassuming, charming guys. They were clearly flirting, but in ways meant to make her laugh rather than to win her affections.

"He failed to mention how handsome you were," she teased, sneaking a peek at Fergus, who was now grinning at their antics.

Finn sighed as if he wasn't surprised to hear that. "He always leaves that part out. Bastard has been wicked jealous of me his entire life."

"Get away from her, Finn," Fergus said. "I want to introduce her to the only one of you clowns who has manners. Aubrey, this is my soon-to-be cousin-in-law, Landon Riggs."

Landon stepped forward and shook her hand politely. "It's nice to meet you. My future bride wanted me to tell you she's bought all your albums, and at some point during this crazy weekend, I hope you'll forgive me if I ask you to sign the covers. They're in my luggage." Landon turned around, looking at Fergus. "Sorry, man. Sunnie wouldn't take no for an answer."

"She never has," Fergus replied.

Aubrey smiled. "I'd be happy to sign her album covers. Fergus has told me a lot about Sunnie. About your whole family, actually."

"What do you mean, 'during this crazy weekend'?" Fergus asked his cousin and friends.

"We wanted to surprise you," Finn responded. "Ailis helped us set it up. We're all here for Landon's bachelor party. Colm and Padraig are visiting with Hunter and Ailis on their bus. Unfortunately, Lochlan and Lucas had to bow out because of work commitments, and Oliver volunteered to stay back and man the bar at the pub with Uncle Tris."

Fergus frowned. "As much as I'd like to take part in a bachelor party, I'm working the whole weekend."

"Oh, we know," Landon said. "That's why we were hoping," he glanced back at Aubrey, "um..."

Apparently, the groom thought she was the boss. "I'd let him have the weekend off, but I have no power over Fergus. He was hired by my record producer. I know this because I've tried to fire him a few times. He won't leave."

Miguel laughed. "That sounds like Fergus. An upright, honest, responsible pain in the ass."

"A pain in the ass who can take *you* down in..." Fergus glanced at Finn, "What was my best time?"

"Last training session, you had Miguel on his ass in three-point-four seconds," Finn helpfully supplied.

"I wasn't ready," Miguel protested. "I *told* you I wasn't ready."

Landon looked at Aubrey. "We knew he couldn't get the weekend off. Ailis told us Fergus wouldn't leave your side. So we were actually thinking that maybe you could join the party tonight. We got a big-ass suite at the same hotel you're staying in and you wouldn't be the only woman there. Ailis and Hunter are coming too."

"What about the strippers?" Aubrey asked, only half-joking, while secretly thrilled by the invite. A night with this group of characters would not only be guaranteed fun, but she liked seeing this side of Fergus. He seemed...younger...more playful around them.

Not that he was old. She'd looked at his personnel file. He was only two years older than her at twenty-eight. But the professional, serious way he held himself gave the impression that he was much older.

"Goddammit," Miguel muttered. "I *told* you she'd be fine with strippers." He looked at her, shaking his head apologetically. "They wouldn't let me hire any."

Landon grinned. "We're going to the concert tonight, Ailis scored us all front-row seats and backstage passes. Then we're going back to the hotel bar, then—when they inevitably kick us out—we're moving the party to the suite. Miguel will, no doubt, provide the wild antics that will have the hotel manager threatening to kick us out and the cops called."

She laughed. "That's a hard invite to pass up."

"Please don't," Finn said. "If you say no, the old stick-in-the-mud over there will bail on us too."

Aubrey looked at Fergus. "Pain in the ass. Stick-in-the-mud. Plain. Your friends know you well."

Fergus shot her a pretend dirty look as the other men cracked up.

"Ailis *said* you were cool," Finn replied, his comment catching her off-guard.

Ailis thought that?

Aubrey was touched. "I've never been to a bachelor party. I'd love to come if you don't think it will put a damper on things."

"A hot, famous rocker chick at my bachelor party?" Landon said. "You've just set me up with bragging rights at the precinct for the rest of my life."

"You're a police officer?" she asked.

"Yep. And for better or worse, Miguel is my partner on the force. We're aware that there's been trouble for you, a stalker." Landon's eyes softened. "We won't let anyone get near you tonight, promise."

Aubrey hoped that promise didn't include Fergus. Because she suspected this evening, surrounded by all these handsome, charismatic men, with their easy laughter and silly banter, not to mention the ungodly amount of tequila she planned to drink, was going to lead her to make some irresponsible decisions.

She couldn't wait.

＊ 8 ＊

Fergus rolled his eyes as Miguel spun Aubrey around in time to the music. They'd set up camp in the hotel bar right after the concert. The place was packed because it hadn't taken long for guests of the hotel to find out Aubrey and Hunter were there. After the initial round of requests for photos and autographs, everyone settled down, thrilled to simply be in the presence of rock stars.

Hunter and Ailis were hanging out by the bar, talking to a few fans.

A couple of guys from Hunter's band had brought their guitars and started jamming. Fergus had anticipated having to deal with the hotel manager, but when he saw the huge crowd ordering drinks at the bar, he announced they'd stay open as long as everyone wanted.

"What a great night," Landon said.

"I didn't realize you'd noticed," Colm teased. "Been texting Sunnie the whole time."

Landon laughed. "Not the whole time. And I can't help it. She's demanding pics of everything. It would have been easier to just let her come."

"Sort of defeats the idea of a bachelor party," Padraig chimed in.

Landon shrugged. It was obvious the man was head over heels in love with Sunnie, too preoccupied with thoughts of her to care much about drinking with a bunch of guys in a hotel bar, bachelor party or not.

"Miguel and Finn are making jackasses of themselves," Fergus grumbled, watching as Finn cut in—again—to steal Aubrey for a dance. Not that she seemed to mind their antics.

Fergus hadn't seen her laugh much the past month, but she'd more than made up for it tonight.

Miguel, annoyed at losing his dance partner once more, took matters into his own hands, claiming the back of Aubrey, the three of them swaying to the music together. Finn didn't appear to mind sharing.

Meanwhile, it was wearing thin on Fergus. Not the dancing or the way the guys flirted with her. He knew that was harmless fun.

He couldn't stop thinking about what had almost happened on the bus this morning. And how anxious he was to get her alone so they could finish what they'd started.

Landon and Padraig excused themselves to grab another drink from the bar, leaving him alone with Colm.

"So...you and Aubrey," his cousin mused.

Fergus frowned. "What about us?"

"You've been staring at her nonstop for the past couple of hours. And not like a bodyguard, or like the rest of these love-struck fools either, but like a man who's already staked a claim."

Fergus shook his head. "I haven't slept with Aubrey."

Colm grinned. "Go ahead and tack the *yet* on there. We both know you're thinking it."

Fergus leaned back and sighed. He hadn't talked about his feelings for Aubrey to anyone. He could have shared with Ailis and Hunter, but until this morning, he'd been determined to fight the attraction.

Now, there was no way he could turn back.

"We kissed this morning. And if you guys hadn't shown up when you had, I wouldn't have given you the same answer to your question about us."

Colm winced. "Bad timing."

Fergus chuckled, then glanced back toward Aubrey, still dancing. "Finn and Miguel. The ultimate cockblock. All damn day."

Fergus hadn't managed to steal a single minute alone with Aubrey since they'd shown up. Whenever she wasn't running through sound checks or in hair and makeup, Miguel and Finn had flanked her, proclaiming she was their girl.

Erick and Rich stopped by the table.

"Hey, F-Fergus. What's up? Who are t-they?" Erick asked, noticing where Fergus's gaze was focused.

"My cousin, Finn, and a friend, Miguel," Fergus replied. "They're in town for a bachelor party this weekend."

"She's having f-fun," Erick said.

Rich laughed. "I'll say. It's a shame those guys only have eyes for each other. Looks like Aubrey's going to be odd guy out tonight."

Erick grinned. "I d-didn't know they were g-gay."

Rich slapped Erick on the back. "I'll tell you how you can tell, Erick," he said as the two men continued to their table.

Colm and Fergus both took a harder look at the dance floor.

"Eyes for each other?" Fergus mumbled.

Colm seemed to be just as taken aback by that comment as him. "You think?"

Fergus shrugged, then studied Finn and Miguel closer. There was nothing overt about their behavior toward each other. For the most part, their attention was totally on Aubrey.

But then...

Fergus saw it. A shared glance. A heated one. It only lasted a second, but it made him wonder.

"Finn only goes out with girls," Colm said.

Fergus nodded. "Yeah, but Miguel is very open about being bi. Maybe—"

"Hey, guys," Hunter said, walking over with Ailis. "We were thinking about moving this party to Landon's suite. Ailis has a little bit of a headache, and I think we've both reached our limit on socializing with strangers. Thought it might be cool if we downsized to just family, so we could visit for a little while."

Fergus nodded. "That's a great idea." He rose from the table. "I'll grab Aubrey, Finn, and Miguel."

"I'll settle the tab and tell Padraig and Landon we're heading out." Colm walked to the bar.

"What's the plan?" Finn asked when Fergus approached, seeing everyone starting to gather near the exit.

"Thought we'd head up to the suite. Give ourselves a little family time. It's nearly three a.m. now."

"Cool." Miguel and Finn thanked Aubrey for the dance, then went to join the others.

"I guess I'll see you in the morning then," she said.

Fergus frowned. "What? You're not coming?"

"You said family time."

He wrapped his arm around her shoulders. "You're included in that."

"But—"

"No buts. We're going to hang out for a little while, then you and I are going back to the room together." Fergus tugged her closer, pressing a kiss on her forehead. "I owe you a punishment, remember?"

She bit her lower lip, but there was no mistaking the desire in her eyes.

"Come on," he said, propelling her toward his family. "You keep looking at me like that and the party ends here."

She lifted her face toward his. "I wouldn't mind saying good night to the others."

Fergus couldn't resist stealing a real kiss. Aubrey met him

halfway, and the peck he'd meant to keep short and sweet, lingered.

It was a pretty public proclamation, kissing her in front of the band and so many members of the crew. There were probably several fans documenting the kiss with their camera phones.

Fergus knew what he was doing. Knew exactly what he was starting here.

Time wasn't on their side. Though Fergus's primary objective from the record company was keeping Aubrey safe, there was no way in hell he could leave her when the tour ended with the stalker still on the loose.

Which meant it was time to up the ante, draw the bastard out. Fergus didn't want any more innocents to suffer. From this point on, he'd be the target.

However, that wasn't the only thing—not even the main thing—driving the kiss.

She was his—and it was time the rest of the world knew it.

Finn and Miguel were both staring at them, wide-eyed, when they broke apart and continued walking toward them.

"Wow. Way to steal our girl," Miguel muttered, though the shit-eating grin on his face proved he was amused by Fergus's obvious display of jealousy.

Finn slapped him on the back. "So, drooling on the client is bad form, but kisses are legit? You're going to have to go over your list of bodyguard do's and don'ts for me after this job ends. I think it might be an interesting list."

"Shut up," Fergus murmured, prompting the others to laugh, including Aubrey.

They crowded onto the elevator, chatting as it climbed. They'd all spent the majority of the day in each other's company, but when two or more members of the Collins family got together, the conversations were endless. So were the laughs.

The next hour passed quickly as the party quieted down, all of them catching up, sharing old family stories with Miguel and Aubrey, Landon finally giving up on trying to relay everything that was happening and looping Sunnie in via FaceTime on his phone, the two of them talking about their plans for the wedding, which was taking place the day after the Fourth of July concert.

They'd picked that date because all the family had plans to attend Hunter's concert, so everyone would already be in Baltimore. Sunnie had insisted on having every single member of the family at her nuptials, so she'd chosen the date with care, even if it meant no rehearsal dinner the night before. According to Sunnie, the reception would be so epic, no one would mind one less event.

Ailis and Hunter excused themselves first, Ailis's headache growing worse.

He, Aubrey and Padraig shared one of the couches, and he listened quietly as Padraig explained that he was a widower when Aubrey noticed his wedding ring and asked about his wife. Fergus had only met Mia a couple of times, but he'd heard many, many things about her from Pop Pop, his family and Padraig. Though she'd only been a Collins for a very short time—less than a year—she'd had a huge impact on his family.

Fergus was glad to see that Padraig could talk about Mia without quite as much sadness these days. Time appeared to be healing Padraig's wounds, though Fergus suspected the pain of losing her would never fully subside.

Aubrey listened, and even wiped away a tear as Padraig talked about his own wedding day. Fergus had been stationed in Afghanistan, unable to make it to the wedding, so a lot of what his cousin shared about the event was new to him as well.

Finally, they rose, everyone ready for bed. It had been fairly tame as far as bachelor parties went, but from the smile on Landon's face, it was obvious it had been the perfect night.

Fergus and Aubrey walked to the elevator hand in hand, kissing once they were alone inside. As the doors slid open, he led her to her suite. Then he stopped short.

On the floor outside the door was another rose.

However, unlike the others, this one was crushed, as if someone had tossed it down, then smashed it with the heel of their boot.

Glancing around, Fergus noticed that someone had smashed the video camera on this hall as well.

He'd checked the video feed leading up to someone breaking it the last time the rose had appeared outside her hotel room door. All he'd seen was a man in sunglasses with a ball cap pulled low over his face, the hood of a hoodie pulled over his head. Every part of the man had been covered—head to toe, and he'd worn gloves. There was no way to distinguish him from any other man in the world. He hadn't even been able to discern his race. Fergus had watched the grainy film right up until the man had smashed the camera with a hammer and the video went black.

Fergus knew when he checked the footage here, he'd discover the same.

Aubrey gasped when she spotted the crushed rose. "I don't—"

Fergus grabbed the rose and attached note, quickly opened the door, ushered her inside, and locked the door behind them. He did a thorough scan of the suite, checking even the shower in the bathroom and the closets.

"It's crushed."

"Yeah." Fergus didn't like the fear in her voice as he looked at the flower in his hand.

"There's a note."

There was always a fucking note. He opened it.

He'll never touch you again.

Aubrey dropped down onto the couch, and Fergus could see she was fighting hard not to cry. "Who? They always appear after someone's been hurt."

"I know." He kept waiting for Aubrey to state the obvious, to point out that the crushed rose was clearly a warning for him, but she didn't seem to realize that. "Let me make some calls."

For the next forty-five minutes, Fergus spoke to Marcus, Blair, the head of Hunter's security team, then at her request, he called Colm to make sure the family was safe. That was when he realized that was where Aubrey's fears had taken her. She mentioned Finn and Miguel dancing with her. His chest had been tight with anxiety until Colm assured him they were all fine and would remain in their suite the rest of the night.

He considered telling her his theory on the rose, but she was too wired at the moment, pacing the living room. He'd talk to her about it tomorrow after she'd managed some sleep and had a little less tequila in her system.

She wasn't drunk—neither of them was—but she wasn't seeing the whole picture either.

From his calls, he'd learned that no one had seen Doug. And according to the security team, the footage from the hallway camera revealed the same man they'd seen in the first video. He'd concealed himself well again.

Most importantly, for Aubrey's peace of mind, everyone on the crew had been accounted for, and no one had been hurt.

"Fergus..." she started, dropping down onto the couch.

He sank down next to her, taking her hand. "It's okay, Aubrey. I've got everyone on high alert. If he *was* planning to hurt someone, it's going to be harder now. Marcus has called the local police and reported the incident. They're sending a couple of officers over to check things out and stand guard on this hall. I don't know what else we can do right now."

She squeezed his hand. "There isn't anything. You've taken care of it all. You always take care of it. Fergus, I don't know how I ever—"

She stopped short, but Fergus could fill in the blanks. He knew why she wouldn't let herself say the rest.

He had spent the better part of the day thinking about her request this morning for hard, rough, raw. That was exactly what he wanted as well.

But Aubrey was mistaken in her belief that *any* kind of sex would allow her to remain distant from him.

He'd considered explaining that to her this morning...then realized he wanted to show her.

Wanted to push the hardest limit she had.

Trust.

Fergus wanted it, and he was prepared to force the issue.

Now.

"Aubrey. Bedroom."

Aubrey's heart started to race when Fergus stood, tugging her up as well. She'd fantasized about this moment nonstop since this morning. Hell, if she was being honest, she'd indulged in racy daydreams about the man since the first day she'd lain eyes on him.

He released her hand briefly, picking up the shopping bag he'd returned to the hotel with this afternoon.

"Pajamas?" she asked.

He shook his head. "While Miguel, Landon and Finn were guarding you earlier—"

"Guarding me?"

"They stood watch backstage during your sound checks while I ran some errands."

They'd had some issues with the soundboard, so that task had taken twice as long as usual. Aubrey hadn't even realized Fergus was gone. It spoke to the level of trust he had in his family and friends that he'd left her alone.

"Where did you go?" she asked.

"Aubrey. You told me what you wanted this morning. If you've changed your mind about that, say the word and we'll take off our clothes, crawl between those covers and make love all night."

Her chest tightened the second he said the word *love*, and she fought to catch her breath.

There was very little Fergus missed. He recognized her distress and cupped her cheek with one hand, the other still holding the bag. "Okay," he said. "So the plan remains the same. Rough, raw."

His words didn't help her breathing, but the constriction was no longer based on panic. He knew exactly what to say to turn her terror to arousal. No small feat.

She nodded.

"Take off your clothes, Aubrey."

His request caught her off-guard. They'd done nothing more than kiss a few times, and he'd touched her breasts exactly once. She licked her lips nervously. "What about *your* clothes?"

He crossed his arms, his expression stern. He didn't bother to answer. It wasn't as if he needed to. She could tell he wasn't going to repeat his request or allow her to stall.

"Your safe word is Rottweiler. If it's too much and you need a break, say that, and we'll stop, talk, reevaluate. Don't use it unless you mean it."

She smiled, despite her anxiousness. He'd chosen a word that would make her feel in control, even as she longed to let go of it.

Aubrey couldn't quite believe she was doing this.

"Rottweiler," she whispered. "That works."

He raised one eyebrow, reminding her that he'd given her an order. She'd seen evidence of his military training countless times since he'd started serving as her bodyguard, but none so much as now.

This Fergus was so commanding, so stern, so freaking sexy.

She reached for the hem of her shirt and pulled it over her head. His gaze lowered, looking at her with obvious appreciation.

Aubrey tried to decide which article of clothing to take off next. Bra or jeans? Which would leave her feeling less revealed, less vulnerable?

She opted for the jeans, unfastening them, then slowly pushing them down. She bent over to tug off her boots and socks, then kicked away the denim.

Then she stood upright, sucking in a deep breath as she resisted the urge to lift her arms and cover herself.

It was a strange desire. Aubrey had limitless confidence when she was onstage, performing before thousands of people. Some of her costumes skirted the lines of indecency—slits to her hips, low-cut fronts, plunging backlines that nearly revealed her ass. She wore all those things easily, no shyness, no reserve.

But now, standing before an audience of one—Fergus—she felt uncertain of herself, afraid of not being good enough. It wasn't a new fear for her—she'd suffered the same through most of her childhood, constantly criticized by her mother, then jilted by all three of her lovers.

"You're the most beautiful woman I've ever seen, Aubrey. Stunning. Perfect."

She smiled at his praise. Once again, it felt as if he could read her thoughts, and as always, he knew exactly how to put her at ease, how to bolster her wavering confidence.

At least, he did. Until he said, "Keep going."

She closed her eyes as she reached behind her back, unhooking her bra. She held on to the cups as long as she could before finally allowing the lace to fall to the floor.

"Look at me, Aubrey."

Her cheeks felt warm. God. Was she blushing? She *never* blushed.

She raised her gaze and saw the naked desire in his. He hadn't lied. He did think she was beautiful. Perfect.

If only...

She reached for her panties and shimmied them over her hips to the floor, stepping out of them.

Her eyes remained locked on his because he gave her the strength, the courage to keep going.

"Turn around. Full circle. Slowly."

She took an unsteady breath, then did as he requested. She'd never had a lover take such delight in simply looking at her.

Of course, she'd never had a lover like Fergus. She was twenty-six and she'd slept with three men, all of them cut from the same Doug-like pattern. Weak men who seemed content to ride the waves rather than direct the sails.

She knew exactly two sexual positions—missionary and doggie style. Something told her Fergus knew a hell of a lot more.

Once she'd completed the three-sixty, she faced him again.

"I'm going to ask you one more time, Aubrey. Are you sure this is what you want?"

She nodded, zero hesitation. Absolutely nothing in her life was certain, everything up in the air or in litigation. She'd gotten nothing she'd ever asked for.

Until now.

Until him.

"I'm sure," she said, her voice steadier than she would have expected.

He gave her a ghost of a grin, his first since leading her to the bedroom. "Go to the bed, bend over the edge, facedown. We'll get the punishment out of the way first. If you behave during that, I'll give you a reward."

Her stomach fluttered with excitement as she assumed the position he requested.

She'd never had a father, and while her mother had been over-protective and controlling, it was never in a maternal way. Since she was three, she'd been treated like an employee, never a daughter.

As such, she'd never been spanked. That was another thing on her list of missed childhood events, along with bedtime stories, sleepovers, birthday parties that weren't photo opportunities, and public schooling. Her education had come from tutors between takes.

Fergus followed her, and she shivered—though not from the cold—when he ran his hand along her bare back. Like this morning, he bent his body over hers, the cotton of his T-shirt soft against her skin.

He kissed her cheek, his lips traveling along the side of her face to her ear, down her neck. A breathless giggle escaped when he nipped her shoulder.

There was something exciting about being completely naked in front of a fully dressed man. Of course, there was something to be said for a hot naked guy too. She'd never seen Fergus without a shirt or pants, but she sure as hell had squandered countless hours fantasizing about it.

He stood once more, directly behind her, his hands softly stroking her back, the globes of her ass, tops of her thighs. She loved the feeling of his fingers caressing her, but it wasn't enough.

"You have a beautiful ass," he murmured.

She turned her head to look at him over her shoulder, smiling. That expression faded fast when he raised one hand, bringing it down hard.

She jerked, not expecting it to hurt so much.

Fergus didn't reply to her cry of pain. Instead, he spanked her again, four or five times in quick succession, even as she tried to crawl away.

He bent over, gripping her shoulder with one hand, holding her in place as the spanking continued.

Her ass was on fire, stinging. She kept struggling, but he didn't relent.

Why would he?

She knew the way to make him stop. It was as simple as one word.

She didn't say it.

"Why am I punishing you?" he asked, his hand resting on her sore bottom.

"Because I put myself in danger."

"How?"

"By trying to hide from you. Leaving the bus without telling you."

Fergus sat down next to her on the mattress. "Promise me, Aubrey. Promise you won't do that again. I can't stand not knowing if you're safe."

She hadn't expected that admission from him. He was hired to protect her. It was his job. Knowing that he truly worried about her touched her more than she cared to admit.

She pushed herself to her side, facing him. "I promise."

And she meant it.

Finally, he returned her smile, then he narrowed his eyes. "Did I say you could move?"

She shook her head and forced herself back down. Her ass really did hurt. She wasn't sure she could take much more.

Fergus's hands roamed gently over her ass cheeks. "So warm," he murmured. He shifted again, but this time, rather than standing, he knelt behind her, his lips kissing away the hurt, turning the sting to pure sensual sensation.

He nudged her legs apart, his fingers exploring deeper, lower.

She gasped when he touched her clit, finding it on the first pass. There was a lot to be said for an experienced lover. Aubrey had to guide Doug to her clit every single time. And even then, he only gave it a few passing strokes before he forgot about it and moved on.

Fergus appreciated its importance. He continued to kiss her bottom as his finger toyed with, even pinched her clit. Aubrey began thrusting toward him, wiggling as she searched for more. She'd never been this aroused, this hungry.

"Please," she said.

"We've got miles to go, Aubrey. Be patient."

Miles? She didn't like the sound of that. She was ready now.

"Fergus, please," she persisted.

"Behave or I'll spank you again."

That didn't feel like as much of a threat as it had earlier. The previous stinging fire had eased into a tantalizing heat that warmed her from the outside in. His lips—though warm—felt cool against her skin, and they only served to increase her desire more.

Fergus gave her clit several firmer strokes that had her back arching in delight, then he slid one finger inside her.

"Yes," she hissed, as he thrust it in and out several times. Her pussy clenched against it—and before she even realized what was happening, she came.

Fergus's finger remained lodged within her, but he stopped moving as waves of pleasure washed through her.

"You came," he said as the tremors subsided and every muscle in her body relaxed.

She couldn't read his tone, couldn't tell if he was surprised or annoyed.

Aubrey lifted her head, glancing back at him. "Um. Sorry?"

He chuckled. "Don't apologize. You just..." His smile grew wider. "You didn't make me work very hard for it."

She giggled. "I'll try harder next time."

"Don't. Let yourself go, Butterfly. You're free here with me."

A lump formed in her throat, and she blinked several times, willing away the tears.

Before she could reply, Fergus gave her a light slap on the ass.

"Up on the bed," he said. "Hands and knees."

She crawled to the middle of the mattress, peering at him curiously as he picked up the bag he'd carried to the room.

Aubrey frowned when he pulled out a blindfold. She'd been expecting something a lot more exciting.

Fergus placed his knee on the bed next to her, and her chest tightened, panic closing in. She shook her head as he attempted to cover her eyes with the soft material.

"Hold still."

"No," she said. "Please."

Fergus didn't stop, and she belatedly realized why.

"Rot—"

She stopped herself from saying the word, even though she wanted to.

Fergus paused for the briefest of moments, waiting to see if she'd finish the word. When she didn't, he continued to put the blindfold over her eyes, resting a comforting hand at the nape of her neck once it was in place. "Breathe, Aubrey," he said soothingly.

She tried to draw in air, but her lungs constricted.

"Why don't you like the blindfold?" he asked. "Is it because of the nightmare?"

Aubrey shook her head, wishing she weren't so stupid, so weak, so suspicious of everyone. "No. I don't want..." She paused. She didn't want to tell him the real reason.

"Tell me, Aubrey. And keep in mind, I'll know if you're lying."

She was tempted to pull the blindfold off. It would be easier to talk to him if she could see his face. "I don't—"

She blew out a long breath and forced the truth out.

"I don't want you to take pictures of me."

She hated that *that* was where her fears took her, but with the blindfold on, she wouldn't be able to see him, wouldn't know what he was doing that he could use against her later.

"Here."

She felt him press something cool and smooth into her hand. "What—"

"It's my phone. Hold on to it for me."

"I...you...aren't mad at me?"

She could hear the smile in his voice. "Aubrey. I know how hard it is for you to give your trust to someone. You've been hurt a lot in the past. All I'm asking you for is the chance to prove that I won't let you down. Okay?"

Aubrey nodded and sniffed. Every sweet thing he said made

her want to cry, not tears of sadness, but of hope and happiness. "Okay," she whispered thickly.

"Blindfold stays on unless you plan on finishing that word." His voice was deep, confident, the tone of a man who expected to have his wishes obeyed.

With his phone in her hand, every part of her tensed up again...with arousal rather than fear. "No. I'm okay."

He used the hand still on the back of her neck to push her upper body toward the mattress. She shifted from holding herself up with her hands to her elbows.

"Such a pretty ass," he murmured, stroking skin that was still sensitive from his spanking.

She heard the crinkle of the bag once more. Without the ability to see, her other senses heightened and she tried to figure out what he was doing through sound.

Aubrey jerked slightly when something cool and wet touched her ass.

Oh God.

She trembled as Fergus pressed the tip of one finger into her anus.

"I don't...I never..."

"Shhh," he soothed. "It's okay, Butterfly. I'm not going to do anything that hurts."

She laughed breathlessly. "You realize that spanking hurt."

He chuckled. "That was supposed to be a punishment. But the fact that you came right on the heels of it tells me it fell short of that."

"I liked it," she confessed. "I didn't expect—"

Her words were abruptly cut off when Fergus pushed his whole finger into her ass.

"Oh my God," she said, the words more air than sound.

"You like this too." Fergus didn't ask. He didn't need to. Somehow, even though they'd only known each other a short time, he could read her—all of her—without words.

"Yes."

He moved the finger in and out several times, adding more lubrication before sliding in a second finger. He stretched her just to the point of pain, but there was something so wicked about being touched this way that distracted her from any discomfort.

More than that, it fueled her desire, made her want to try everything. She'd never explored her sexuality, never trusted anyone enough to expand on her knowledge, her experiences in the bedroom.

With Fergus...she did.

That realization shook her.

But he didn't give her time to consider the implications or fall prey to the inevitable panic attack that was bound to ensue.

His fingers disappeared—and something harder touched her anus.

"What—"

"Butt plug," he answered before she could ask the question.

Wow. Fergus definitely didn't let the grass grow under his feet. He'd obviously considered what he wanted from her, and now he was making it happen.

She gasped as he pushed the thickest part of the toy inside her. It felt forbidden...and really fucking hot. Aubrey moved one hand to her clit, intent on stroking herself. She'd already come once, but her body apparently forgot about that. She was close...again.

She'd barely managed more than a glancing touch when Fergus gripped her hand, pulling it away and using it to flip her to her back. He came over her, and she realized he was still fully dressed. She reached for the hem of his T-shirt, anxious to pull it off. She wanted skin on skin. If she couldn't see him, at least she could feel him.

Fergus shoved her hand away again.

"Hey," she protested.

"You aren't in control here, Aubrey. Do as I say—*only* what I say. Do you understand?"

"I want you naked."

"I'll take that as a no. You don't understand."

"Please, Fergus! I'm so close. Too close. It hurts. I need—"

"I know what you need, Aubrey."

His reassurance calmed her. Because he really *did* know. He actually knew better than she did.

"Good," he murmured as she stilled.

The bag crinkled again and she smiled, something he clearly noticed.

"So fucking perfect," he whispered.

He'd said that several times tonight already, and each time, it washed through her like warm water on ice-cold skin. It made her believe in things she hadn't let herself feel in a very long time.

Something heavy and cold snapped around one of her wrists. Then he lifted both her arms above her head, clasping them together with handcuffs. These didn't feel like the fur-covered, fun kind sold in sex shops. These were the real deal.

"They're my cuffs. I'm not attaching you to the headboard. I just want you to get used to the feeling of being bound. Next time I get you in my bed, you're going to be completely tied, helpless to move, to do anything other than take what I give you."

She shivered excitedly. "You could do that tonight."

He laughed softly. "No. You're not ready for that."

Aubrey recalled her fear of the blindfold and realized he might be right. She wiggled slightly until her shoulder bumped against his phone, lying right next to her on the mattress.

"Keep your hands above your head."

She nodded in acknowledgement, struggling to speak when she felt him leave the bed again. There was no mistaking the sound of him undressing, and she wished he'd take off the blindfold.

There was another crinkling, this sound different from that of the bag.

A condom.

Then his weight on the bed again. He resumed his previous position above her. And then, she got her wish.

He tugged the blindfold off.

"I was going to leave it on, but I need to see those pretty blue eyes of yours when I come inside you for the first time."

Aubrey started to lift her arms, but the weight of the cuffs reminded her of his command that she keep them there. She was beneath him, naked, her position one of ultimate surrender.

In a lot of ways, that was what this felt like. She'd given up the battle, let him take her.

When he shifted, lifting her knees and placing them over his shoulders, the head of his cock touched her clit, and every part of her relaxed, then tensed.

He pressed in slowly until he reached the hilt, then pulled out again, thrusting in and out in a steady pace meant to give her body time to adjust to his invasion.

Fergus was a well-endowed man. With the extra pressure of the butt plug still in her ass, Aubrey wasn't sure she'd ever felt so full. Every minute move he made tweaked and touched some previously unnoticed part of her. She was struggling to keep up.

"So tight," she said.

He grinned. "I think that's my line."

She laughed softly, amazed how Fergus could make something this intense, this powerful, fun as well.

He continued to move inside her as Aubrey's climax built slowly. She'd been on the precipice earlier, thinking her orgasm eminent. He was purposely drawing it out, making her want more. So much more.

"Faster," she begged, the word accompanied with a moan of pleasure when his cock hit a spot inside her that had her seeing stars. "God! Yes."

"You're going to give me two more orgasms, Aubrey."

She shook her head, even though she knew that response was

futile. Fergus would take what he wanted, regardless of her response. And she'd love every fucking second of it.

His pace increased as he thrust harder. Her back arched as she exploded, crying out loudly. Fergus kept pumping inside her throughout her orgasm, causing it to last longer, grow even more powerful.

Aubrey called out his name, over and over, her body shaking.

Once her climax waned, Fergus withdrew.

She lay limp on the bed, only vaguely aware that he hadn't come yet. Then she recalled his command. *Two more orgasms.*

"I can't do that again," she said, breathlessly. "It's all too good. It'll kill me."

He chuckled, but didn't take her words seriously. "Roll over, Butterfly. I want to see that pretty pink ass again."

She tried, but her bones had turned to jelly. Fergus helped her, dragging her ass up until her knees were beneath her, supporting her. She didn't bother to lift her head from the mattress. She didn't even open her eyes. She was awash in a sea of bliss and in no hurry to come back to shore.

Until Fergus plowed back inside her with all the force and speed she'd wanted a few moments earlier. However, her inner muscles were too overstimulated.

"God!" she yelled, shocked when her exhausted body started to respond to his rough claiming.

There was no other way to describe the way Fergus was taking her. His fingers clenched her hips tightly, dragging her backwards for every powerful forward thrust. He was deeper than he'd been before, this position making her feel doubly fucked as he wasn't only taking her pussy, but slightly nudging the butt plug in and out of her ass as well.

Aubrey's fingers tightened, scratching at the sheets as she sought purchase. Her wrists were still bound, the cuffs clanging with each inward thrust.

She came without warning, tossed over a cliff she never even saw coming. Fergus followed her over, his thrusts reduced to slow, hard jerks as he climaxed, her name on his lips.

"Aubrey. Beautiful Aubrey…"

They remained locked together for several moments, neither of them willing to be the first to break the connection.

Fergus shifted, lifting her slowly, until her back was pressed against his chest, his arms engulfing her, taking her breasts in his large hands.

He'd paid them very little attention during the foreplay, but he seemed determined to make up for that now. His lips slid along the side of her neck, just behind her ear, and she realized they'd barely kissed either.

"Hold still." He drew her knees apart and for a second, she panicked, thinking perhaps he intended to do it all over again.

She'd never had three orgasms in one night, and while she'd joked about it killing her, there was no way a fourth wouldn't do her in for real.

When she felt his fingers at the rim of her ass, she recalled the plug. She held her breath as he tugged it out.

"I'm going to put that inside you before a concert one night, then watch you perform, making sure all you can think about as you sing is me."

Aubrey shivered, loving the idea of that. She didn't bother to tell him he'd been consuming her thoughts while she was onstage for weeks.

He drew a key from the bag, unlocking the handcuffs and placing them on the nightstand.

"Lay down, sweetheart. I'll be right back."

She hadn't had much opportunity to look at his naked form before. As he walked away from her, toward the bathroom, she decided Fergus had the greatest ass she'd ever seen.

When he returned, she noticed he'd disposed of the condom and had splashed water on his face, a few drops clinging to his beard. She'd been looking at him for a month solid, and even now, his stunning good looks still had the power to take her breath away. He was wasted as a bodyguard, more suited for what she'd first believed true—he'd make a killing as a model.

She scooted over to make room for him in the bed, reaching behind her when his phone poked her in the back. She handed it back to him with a sheepish grin.

Fergus lay down next to her, turning it on and opening his photos. "No nude pics," he said, offering her the proof. She laughed—before her eyes landed on the last one he'd taken.

She took the phone away from him, studying the shot of her dancing with Miguel and Finn. Her head was thrown back as she laughed, both men grinning widely.

Fergus chuckled at the picture. "Those guys are too much."

There was no jealousy in his voice, nothing but genuine affection. "You're lucky," she said. "You have an incredible family."

Fergus nodded. "I do. When we get to Baltimore, I'll introduce you to the rest of them. My mom will love you."

She smiled. "Might be nice to have a mom love me for once." The words came out flippant, and she'd meant them as a joke. One that fell short. She regretted saying them when Fergus's brows furrowed.

"You don't talk about your mom much. I know she's a despicable person, but there's a part of me that hopes she was kind to you at some point."

She shook her head. "Sorry. No luck there. Mom was fifteen when she got pregnant. Her parents kicked her out of the house, so she dropped out of school, moved in briefly with the sperm donor—some twenty-five-year-old truck driver she'd hooked up with at some random party one night after she'd snuck out. I get the impression that while she was pretty smart, my mom was also a party girl, drinking, doing drugs, sleeping around with older guys."

"You never considered looking for your dad?"

Aubrey shook her head. "No. He kicked my mom out before I was even born. She dragged me around from one friend's house to the next, imposing on each of them as long as she could before they kicked her out too. When I was three, she sent my picture in to some beautiful baby contest. The prize was an all-expense-paid trip to L.A. so I could star in some stupid commercial. Mom hooked up with the sleazy guy producing the commercial, deciding I was destined for fame. We never went back home. We stayed in L.A."

"Did you like acting?"

Aubrey shrugged. "It was okay. I was three when I started. It's not like I ever had a chance to think about it or choose it. It was just the way things always were. My mom landed most of my commercial deals on her back or her knees. Something she brought up countless times in the past few years. Apparently, I'm supposed to be grateful for her efforts on my behalf, not suing her for stealing every dime I ever made. She's a master manipulator and user."

"How the hell did she end up with Doug?"

Aubrey had never talked to *anyone* about finding her mom with Doug. It had actually been her mom who'd leaked that story, selling it to the tabloids to make a few bucks on her daughter's humiliation. It was something her mom fed on, though Aubrey couldn't understand why.

"It's sort of a game she plays." Even as she said it, Aubrey's stomach clenched. Was she really going to tell Fergus the secret she'd never shared? What would he say? Would he look at her differently?

"Game?"

She shrugged, hoping he'd let the conversation end here. Fergus reached for her, wrapping his arm around her shoulders, tugging her closer, until her head rested on his chest.

"What game?" he asked again.

"I haven't had a lot of boyfriends."

"You told me that."

"My mom's slept with all of them."

Fergus pulled away, lifting her face to his, his hand on her chin. "*What?*"

"I lost my virginity to the actor who played Prince Alexander. I was eighteen, Brett was twenty. I was head over heels in first love and certain we were going to have the fairy-tale Hollywood romance. My mom was thirty-three and, much as it pains me to say it, gorgeous. She'd been putting my money to good use, with a nose job, boob job, tanning, blonde highlights, sexy clothes, you name it. Whenever she walked into a room, she had this commanding presence that caught everyone's attention. And I knew Brett looked at her whenever she walked by. Why not? She was beautiful, rich, and had a reputation as a wild lover."

"You caught them together?"

Aubrey shook her head. "No. He confessed to the affair."

"So this guy took your virginity, then slept with your *mom?*"

"Not immediately, but yeah, eventually. I've always sort of thought of my mother as the evil stepmom in *Snow White*. She's vain, the type who has to be the center of attention. Anytime the spotlight stayed on me too long, she found a way to punish me for it."

"Jesus. What a fucking bitch. Candace Summers better steer clear of me."

Aubrey smiled at his muttered curse. It actually made her feel better. "I hooked up with one of the writers on the show about a year after breaking up with Brett, then I caught *him* with my mom in my dressing room. She was bent over my makeup table, and he was taking her from behind. The asshole said she was blackmailing him, telling him she'd have him fired if he didn't fuck her. I have no idea if that was true or not, but I left the show after that, determined to break all ties with my mom. That's when I discovered I was nearly broke. I met Doug a couple years after...and foolishly thought everything would be different. It wasn't."

"I don't know what to say," he said after a few quiet moments. "I spent enough time in the military to know there's true evil in the world. I hate that you were subjected to it from the one person who should have loved you more than all others."

He kissed her gently. "I wish I could take away every bad thing she ever did to you."

Aubrey wasn't sure how, but with those few words, it felt as if that was something he could actually do. After just talking to him, all those memories that had caused her immeasurable pain seemed to hurt a little less now.

Fergus wrapped his arm around her tighter, tugging her even closer. His hugs were warm, soft, safe.

She tried to push that last thought away. There were only two weeks left on this tour, and she'd learned a long time ago that nothing lasted forever.

Aubrey needed to remember that, to hold on to it.

This time was amazing, wonderful.

Fleeting.

10

Fergus glanced at his phone screen and smiled. He'd texted his mother several times over the past month, but he hadn't had a chance to speak to her because their grueling tour schedule kept him hopping.

He and Aubrey had slept until nearly three in the afternoon, something he probably hadn't done since he was a teenager. Of course, considering they'd been up until sunrise, talking and kissing, it was hardly surprising.

If he'd had his way, they'd still be in that bed and he would be buried deep inside her. Sex with Aubrey had been better than every fantasy he'd conjured over the last few weeks.

She was vulnerable in a way that made him want to care for her, feisty in a way that made him want to punish her, and there was no denying her sexual appetites ran parallel to his.

She was made for him.

Now he just had to find a way to convince *her* of that, as well as earn her trust—and catch a crazy stalker.

Piece of cake, he thought sarcastically, snickering to himself.

He was at his usual post outside her bus as Aubrey sat inside, doing an interview for an entertainment magazine.

He answered the phone. "Hi, Mom."

"Fergus," she said. "It's good to hear your voice. I've gotten spoiled ever since you left the Army, talking to you every few days. A month is too long."

"I should have called before now," he said, grinning at her motherly nag. He recalled Aubrey's comments about her mother, which made him aware he didn't appreciate his loving mom nearly enough.

"Finn keeps us up to date. I thought I'd check to make sure everyone was alive after the bachelor party last night."

Fergus laughed. "We survived, though I suspect there are more than a few Collins men sleeping off some headaches this afternoon."

"I would expect nothing less of you idiots," she joked. "Your dads were sorry they couldn't get away from work to join the fun, but they've got a huge project to complete and the weather hasn't been cooperating. I swear it's rained every single day since you left."

"Then I'm glad I'm not there. I hate the rain. Nothing but bright sunshine here in Houston."

"Nice of you to rub it in. And how is your pretty rock star?"

"She's fine," he said, aware that was a very boring answer to describe Aubrey.

"Mmm-hmmm," his mother hummed, clueing him in to the fact that she'd called for a reason. There was no way any of his cousins would have called his mom to tell her about him and Aubrey. They respected his privacy, and would also understand his desire to tell his parents about Aubrey when he was ready. Plus, they'd all been hungover as hell, and he doubted any of them were alert enough to call home for any reason.

As he and Aubrey had been leaving the hotel this morning, they'd run into Ailis, who'd reported that while the whole gang had gotten up and consumed a huge brunch, they'd gone straight back to bed after, resting up for tonight.

Aubrey and Hunter were performing two sold-out shows in Houston. Ailis had gotten the guys tickets for both nights, but while his cousins would all return to the hotel afterwards—probably for part two of the bachelor party—he, Aubrey, Ailis and Hunter would climb back on the buses to head to the next city.

Fergus figured Mom would get to the point eventually, so he said, "She's on the bus doing an interview right now."

"Oh. So, am I to understand that you're going to let me find out about the two of you through the tabloids?"

"What are you talking about?"

"Riley tagged me on a picture she saw on Instagram this morning. Apparently, it's making the rounds on social media."

Fergus frowned. "What picture?"

"It's of you and Aubrey kissing in the hotel bar last night."

Fergus wasn't completely surprised to discover that someone had snapped a picture of that. There had been a slew of fans around. However, he hadn't expected it to make that much of a splash so quickly.

"There's a caption on it."

"Oh?" Fergus wasn't sure he wanted to know what it said.

"Yep. It says 'Aubrey Summers, recently jilted by her fiancé, has found a new sweet flame, her current hunky bodyguard.'"

"No name?"

"Not yet."

Fergus sighed. "Mom, listen, I understand how this looks. It's unprofessional, and I suspect this will be a smear on the company's reputation—"

"Do you care for her?"

Of *course* his mother didn't give a damn about the implications for his business. Instead, she was concerned about his heart.

"I do." He was struggling to believe how fast and far he'd fallen. Their time together had been short, but the truth remained...he cared for her deeply.

"I'm glad to hear that. What happens when the tour is over?"

Leave it to Mom to ask the hard questions, the ones he couldn't find the answers to himself. "I don't know. This is all pretty new."

"I see. Well, at the risk of sounding like Pop, if it's meant to be, it will be."

Fergus chuckled. "Well done, Mom. You nailed a classic Pop Pop-ism."

"I suspect he'll probably call you up at some point to offer his own take on the news. No doubt Riley's shown everyone at the pub that picture. Apparently, she's a pretty big Aubrey Summers fan."

"She probably couldn't escape that fate. According to Finn, he, Darcy, and Sunnie watched *Sweet Flames* pretty much nonstop when they were younger."

"You still have a couple of weeks to see where things go. And then you'll be back in Baltimore—hopefully to stay this time."

"Baltimore is home, Mom. That'll never change."

"By the way, your tux for the wedding is here and ready to go."

Fergus smiled. While Finn was serving as Landon's best man, he and Miguel were on tap as the groomsmen. "Looking forward to it. And glad to be out of town these next two weeks. I can only imagine how insane Sunnie is driving everyone."

Mom laughed. "Well, she's not Bridezilla, but like her mother, she has some fairly eccentric ideas for the ceremony and reception. It will certainly be a fun night."

"I'm sure it will."

"I'll let you get back to work, Fergus. Your fathers send their love. You can probably expect texts from both of them later. I'll warn you, Killian took one look at the picture and said, 'That's it. There's our future daughter-in-law.' I have no idea what he saw in the picture that Justin and I missed, but we're both blaming it on his Collins genetics—the ingrained part that makes all of you hopeless romantics."

"Not all of us. Colm still refers to falling in love and settling down as the Collins curse."

"He'll fall the hardest of all," Mom joked.

"I'll keep an eye out for the texts. It was good to talk to you, Mom."

"Love you, beautiful boy."

He smiled at her nickname for him. The fact that he was a grown man who eclipsed her by a good foot never changed the fact that, in her eyes, she would always see her beautiful boy.

"Love you too. See you in a couple weeks."

They said their goodbyes just as the door to the bus opened and the reporter stepped off, giving him an overly interested look.

Aubrey stood behind the man, and he could see from her expression she was forcing a smile.

Fergus stepped onto the bus once the man was gone.

"What's wrong?" he asked.

"I don't know how to tell you this, but—"

"There's a picture of us kissing last night making its way around social media."

She nodded, surprised. "You're not upset?"

He shook his head. "I initiated that kiss, Aubrey. In public. In a bar where we were surrounded by your fans and the crew."

It appeared that hadn't occurred to her. "Why did you do that?"

Fergus paused, considering his answer. Aubrey still hadn't seemed to figure out that he'd been trying to draw the stalker out, to put himself in the line of fire. But when it came down to it, that wasn't the most important reason he'd had for kissing her. After everything they'd shared last night, there was one truth that mattered more. "Let's just say my male ego overrode my common sense. I wanted every man in that bar to know you were mine."

"Wow," she said, laughing. "Caveman much?"

He pulled her into his arms, kissing her. "I am unapologetically caveman."

"The reporter asked about the picture."

"What did you say?"

She gave him a rueful grin. "I didn't have a clue what to say. I told him the interview was supposed to focus on the tour, and I didn't intend to discuss my personal life with him."

Fergus could just imagine her whipping out that haughty diva voice she'd used on him when he'd first started as her bodyguard. "Good answer."

She gave him an adorable wink. "This ain't my first rodeo."

He kissed her again, this one longer, deeper, his hands drifting from her waist to her breasts. He hadn't spent enough time enjoying them last night. That was something he intended to make up for when he got her back in bed tonight.

Joel was in for a surprise when they hit the road again. The bus driver was losing his shotgun partner. For the rest of the tour, Fergus had every intention of sharing Aubrey's bed, putting the remaining time to good use as he tried to win her trust...and her heart.

Hearing his dad's comment about Aubrey had instantly sparked a desire in him he'd been suppressing. He wanted to continue seeing her after the tour was over, wanted to see if the two of them could make something real, something lasting together.

There was a knock at the door. Aubrey broke the kiss with a regretful groan.

"Shit. That will be Blair. It's time for the sound check."

"Okay. Come on."

They stepped off the bus to find Blair chatting with Finn, Miguel, and Landon.

"Hey, guys," Aubrey said, offering all three men a friendly hug, laughing when Miguel held on extra-long.

"How are you feeling today?" Fergus asked them.

Finn shook his head. "Rough. After you two left, Miguel

dragged out another bottle of tequila and the night took a bad turn."

Fergus winced. "I'm sure it did."

Miguel showed no signs of remorse. "Had to drown my sorrows in *something*. You got the girl and left me with your damn cousins and no strippers."

"Ms. Summers," Blair said. "I'm afraid they need you now."

"Oh yeah. Sorry to run, guys, but I'm due onstage for a sound check. Want to come watch?"

All three men nodded so they headed toward the arena.

Marcus stopped them at the door. "Fergus. You got a minute? There's an issue with the security detail that I'd like to discuss with you."

Fergus frowned. "Aubrey needs to do her sound check."

"We can keep an eye on her," Landon offered, understanding Fergus's reluctance to leave Aubrey unescorted.

"What could be safer than two cops?" Miguel added.

"And me," Finn added.

"You're the one we're protecting her from," Landon joked.

"I'll be fine," Aubrey said, linking her arms with Miguel and Finn. "Every woman backstage is going to be jealous when they see my hot entourage."

Fergus nodded. "I'll be right behind you."

Marcus waited until they were out of earshot. "Thanks for hanging back, Fergus."

"What's the problem?"

"Couple of things. I didn't want to alarm Aubrey, but a couple of the crew saw Doug leaving the arena a little while ago. They alerted the security guards, who tried to catch him, but I swear the guy is slipperier than an eel. There's no way he's getting backstage without help."

They'd determined that already. What they couldn't figure out was who was helping him.

"Dammit," Fergus muttered. "I'm tired of always being two steps behind that guy." The fact that Doug, who was eleven donuts short of a dozen, kept eluding him was starting to chafe.

"And then, there's this. One of the stagehands found it a couple of minutes ago, near the stage."

It was another rose with a note. The difference between this and the others was the envelope. Fergus's name was on it.

He opened it quickly, his heart stopping when he read the words, *You'll never touch her again.*

"Shit," Fergus muttered, kicking himself for letting Aubrey out of his sight. If anything happened to her...

He took off for the stage, slowing when he got there and taking a deep breath. Aubrey was doing her usual checks and nothing looked amiss. She turned, smiling when he stepped onto the stage.

Aubrey gave him a curious look when he didn't return her smile. He started to walk toward her—

A loud crack sounded from overhead.

Aubrey's eyes widened as he heard someone yell, "Look out!"

He acted on instinct, diving to the side—just as one of the lighting rigs crashed a few feet away from him, glass shattering everywhere. Sparks flashed, stinging any part of him that wasn't covered.

If he'd taken two more steps toward her, he would have been directly under the rig and probably dead at the moment. The entire strip of lights had to weigh close to a hundred pounds, maybe even two.

Aubrey started toward him, but he held up his hand to stop her.

"Don't, Aubrey! There's too much glass." Mercifully, the thick denim of his jeans protected his legs.

Finn and Miguel, who'd been on the other side of the stage, flanked Aubrey, pulling her out from under the remaining lights as Landon came and helped him up.

"Jesus, man!" Landon was obviously shaken up. "When that thing came down, I thought..."

"Yeah," Fergus said. "Me too."

He could have been killed.

The stage was soon swarmed with crew members and union workers hired by the concert arena, studying the damage. Fergus used his walkie-talkie, demanding that the security team inspect the rig to confirm what he already knew.

He didn't doubt for a second they'd discover the thing had been tampered with.

He made his way backstage, Aubrey racing into his arms, trembling as she clung to him. "It almost hit you," she said, her voice muffled against his shirt.

"I'm okay, Aubrey."

"Listen, man. This place is too crowded. Get Aubrey somewhere secure and we'll stick around. See what we can learn," Landon said.

"There was a rose. By the stage. One of the hands found it. Question them...all of them. Someone had to have seen something."

Until they determined the rest of the area was safe, he wanted Aubrey tucked away somewhere private.

"Come on," he said, holding her tight against him. "We'll go to your dressing room."

They passed Ailis and Hunter in the hallway. "What happened?" Ailis asked.

Fergus jerked his head toward the stage. "A lighting rig fell. Miguel, Landon and Finn are checking it out."

"Jesus," Hunter muttered. "Someone could have been killed."

Fergus didn't bother to say that someone was him. He and Aubrey continued on, not stopping until he'd locked them inside her dressing room.

He leaned against the door, trying to catch his breath. Aubrey didn't give him a chance. She turned, kissing him hard, desperately.

Fergus reacted without thought, gripping her waist and

pushing her backwards, toward the dressing table. Once there, he pulled her T-shirt off and tugged her jeans down.

Aubrey's hands weren't idle as she sought to strip him of his clothing just as quickly. He was shirtless by the time he had her naked. He lifted her onto the table, knocking over all the bottles, her makeup crashing to the floor.

Aubrey unfastened his jeans, briefly distracted by a nick on his arm. She looked up at him, and he wondered for a moment if the two of them were in shock. He felt wild, out of control.

He pulled his cock out, pressing her legs open with his hips. He was buried inside her in one hard, quick thrust.

Gripping her ass, he pulled her to the edge of the dressing table. Aubrey's lips slid from his, placing soft, wet kisses on his shoulder, his chest, her tongue stroking his nipples.

Through it all, Fergus pounded inside her. She leaned back as far as she could, her legs twining around his waist so that she could use her heels to draw him even closer, deeper.

"Harder!" she pleaded. "Need so much more."

He gave her what she wanted because he needed the same. Their bodies slapped out a vicious rhythm as her fingers dug into his arms.

"Please," she begged.

Fergus pulled out, lifting her off the table and turning her around. Their eyes met through their reflection in the mirror. He started to push back in—then stopped.

"Condom. Jesus." He was breathless, fighting to regain his wits.

Aubrey shook her head as she thrust her ass back toward him. "No. Finish now."

"Aubrey."

"I'm safe. Pill. Please, I need—"

He didn't need to hear more. He slammed back inside as she cried out in pleasure. Reaching up, he took a handful of her hair in his fist, tugging until he could see her face once more in the mirror.

Her inner muscles clenched tightly.

"Yes," she hissed. "Pull it harder."

He gave her everything she asked for and more. With his free hand, he reached around her, pinching one of her tight nipples. "Going to buy you nipple clamps," he said, his words broken up by each hard thrust.

"God, yes."

"Can't get enough of you. Never enough."

"Fergus...I'm going to—" That was all she got out before her orgasm hit.

She took him down hard, and he came as well.

He'd never had sex without a condom. Now, he couldn't imagine ever using one with her again.

She was *his*.

"Mine." The unbidden word slipped out.

Maybe if Aubrey had been in a more stable state of mind, his continual assertion that she belonged to him would have freaked her out. This whole thing was too new, and Aubrey was nowhere near ready for what he wanted from her.

Time. Commitment. God willing, a long, long future.

Aubrey remained bent over the table, not stirring as he pulled out of her.

His legs felt like rubber, so he grabbed the dressing table chair and sank down on it, reaching out to stroke her ass.

The touch prompted her to move, to stand upright. She squeezed her thighs together.

Fergus grasped one of her hands, pulling her closer so he could swipe his finger along her slit, touching the wetness there. She shivered in response, still sensitive from her orgasm.

"You could have been killed," she whispered, tears wetting her lashes.

Fergus drew her down on his lap, kissing her gently. "I'm okay."

"Those lights...someone meant for them to fall on you, didn't they?" Aubrey had finally connected all the dots.

The stalker had seen their kiss—and found his new target.

Him.

"It's going to be okay, Aubrey."

His words didn't soothe her. "No. It's not."

"Listen to me," he said again. "It's okay. *I'm* okay. We're going to catch this son of a bitch and see him put behind bars."

She studied his face. "That kiss last night…"

He clenched his teeth, hating the look in her eyes.

"You meant for this to happen."

Fergus sucked in a shallow, shaky breath, then nodded. "I want this guy caught."

"At what cost? You could have been killed."

"I wasn't."

"Fuck that!" she shouted. "Only because of luck. Jesus, Fergus."

"I swore to keep you safe, Aubrey. I'll do whatever it takes. You have to believe that, trust me. Please."

The comfort he hoped to offer wasn't sinking in.

The anger and fear in her eyes abated, but not in a good way. Fergus didn't like the sudden calmness, resolve he saw there. "No one else is going to get hurt because of me."

He narrowed his eyes. "No one is getting hurt because of you now. *None* of this is your fault. Don't ever let me hear you take the blame for this."

She rose slowly, reaching for her T-shirt. He watched her tug it over her head, donning it like a knight wore armor. She was retreating from him.

"Stop it, Aubrey."

She didn't listen. Instead, she pulled on her jeans and slid her sandals back on. "I'm supposed to be in hair and makeup." There was a wooden tone to her voice that pissed him off.

"Are you listening to me?"

She started across the room. He stood up, quickly fastening his pants and pulling his own shirt back on. "Don't open that door, Aubrey. We're not finished here."

He would tie her to the chair and keep her here all night—concert be damned—if that was what it took to convince her she wasn't at fault, that she wasn't going to walk away from this, from *him*, under the guise of keeping him safe.

She kept walking, opening the door.

"Goddammit," he said, marching toward her. She slipped into the hall just before he could reach her.

There were countless people around, and he realized that she'd planned on that audience. He saw Finn, who'd been speaking to Rich, look in their direction. It hadn't taken his cousin—his best friend—more than one glance to see something was wrong.

"Aubrey," Fergus murmured softly. "Get back in the dressing room."

"This is done," she said, her voice loud. "That kiss meant nothing. *You* mean nothing. I'm calling Isaac and requesting a new bodyguard. You can pack your things."

He crossed his arms. She was crazy if she thought this was going to end here.

"I'm not leaving," he said.

She sniffed, the haughty Aubrey from his first days on the job, returning. "Suit yourself. Just know that this is over. I don't need you. I don't want you."

He stepped in front of her, intent on stopping her escape. "Aubrey," he started.

Her eyes met his, her gaze rife with fear and determination.

"Please, listen to me," he said softly.

She shook her head. "Rottweiler," she whispered as she stepped around him, walking away.

He didn't move for five full seconds, then he followed her. The door to the room set up for hair and makeup was closed. Fergus wanted to open it, wanted to walk inside, but he'd seen her face and for the first time in his life, he sensed he'd only be marching into a battle he couldn't win. He wasn't sure how long he stood there, staring at the doorknob, fighting for the courage to open it, but he knew it was long enough to prove he was a coward.

"Fergus."

He turned to see Finn standing next to him. His cousin had seen everything. "I called Colm. Told them about...."

"She thinks she's protecting me." Fergus snorted miserably. "There's some irony for you. I'm her bodyguard, but she's trying to..."

"It's not a good time for either of you to try to make decisions. You're both riding some pretty powerful emotions with that lighting rig falling and all the other shit that's been going down. The guys are with Hunter and Ailis on their bus. Go on. Take a break, buddy, you need one. Be with them for a little while. Talk it out. I'll watch Aubrey while she's in makeup. No one will get to her. I promise."

Fergus didn't want to let her out of his sight, but his feelings —like hers—were too close to the surface. They were clouding his vision. "Finn, she—"

"I know, man. I know what she means to you. I won't let you down."

Fergus walked out of the arena, toward Ailis and Hunter's bus, then changed direction, heading instead toward Aubrey's. He slowed his approach when he saw Colm standing by the door, a flower in his hand.

He looked up as Fergus approached. From the frown on his face, he knew what his cousin was holding.

"Let me guess," Fergus said, "it says 'You'll never touch her again.'"

Colm shook his head. "No." He handed Fergus the card.

There, in the same handwriting as all the other notes, were new words, chilling words.

You'll both pay for this.

Fergus dropped the card and turned back toward the arena.

Colm caught him by the arm. "Fergus."

He tried to shrug off his cousin's grip. "Colm. I have to get to her!"

"We were all headed to the arena to find you when Miguel spotted this. Finn called back and said you were headed this way. Miguel and Landon have gone to help Finn guard her." Then he gave him a rueful grin. "I drew the short straw."

Fergus frowned. "What? Colm, I don't have time for—"

"Wait a second."

"I can't." Fergus's insides were in knots.

"You need a break. Some distance. Some time to think it out. You're too close to this...to her."

"She's in danger," Fergus said, still wanting to run back to the arena.

"So are you."

"I don't care!"

Colm blew out a long breath. "I know you don't. But *we* care about you. Finn heard Aubrey, heard her break things off. He called to tell us she freaked out and pushed you away. She didn't realize what was behind that kiss at the bar last night, did she?"

Fergus rubbed his eyes wearily. Sometimes it was great to have a close family. Sometimes—like now—it was a total pain in the ass. "I appreciate what you're trying—"

Colm chuckled. "No, you don't. But you're going to listen to someone who has some distance from this whole thing, some perspective. You and Aubrey are acting on emotion and all that's doing is putting you both in danger. It's time to play the game smarter."

"What do you mean?"

"This stalker, whoever he is, has fixated on both of you now."

"It was supposed to just be me."

Colm nodded. "I get that. Just like I can see that Aubrey's intentions were good when she staged that public breakup just now."

"Finn acts fast."

"The game has changed. That note proves it. He's not reacting to perceived threats to Aubrey anymore. He's pissed off at *her* now. Is there anyone on the crew you've discounted as the stalker?"

Fergus shook his head, realizing how much he'd let his interest in Aubrey interfere with doing his job. He shouldn't have taken his focus away from the pursuit of the stalker for even one second. Instead, he'd been distracted by her, her pain, her fears, and how much he wanted her.

He should have been devoting every single second to finding the bastard trying to hurt her.

"She pushed me away, Colm."

"So what?"

Fergus snickered. Jesus. The Collins men were all cut from the same cloth. Colm, a dominant man in his own right, didn't see Aubrey's dismissal as anything Fergus couldn't overcome.

"She said the safe word."

"What?" Colm asked.

"I gave her a safe word. She just used it."

Colm frowned. "That's not how it works."

Fergus grinned, despite the fact he didn't find any of this funny. Colm was a lawyer—a no-nonsense guy who saw the world in black and white. He was also a bachelor who hadn't quite perfected the concept of a long-term love affair. As such, his cousin was lacking in firsthand experience regarding women.

He was fully capable of commanding lovers, women there for the night, but he fell short when it came to the compromises required to make a true relationship.

"She's been hurt, Colm. And I don't mean by lovers. Her mother wrecked her in so many ways, I can't even start to explain them. She's spent her entire life feeling as if she meant nothing more than a paycheck. She doesn't understand how amazing, how beautiful, how incredible she is."

Colm rolled his eyes, even though he grinned. "Jesus. You haven't even been back a year and you've already succumbed to the curse."

"You wait, Colm. Wait until you fall. You're going to give it a different name then."

Colm shook his head. "Never going to happen. But we're straying from the topic at hand. Here's what *will* happen. What you're going to make happen. You're going to explain to that headstrong lady of yours exactly what a safe word is for. Then you're going to keep her close, never let her out of your sight. She'll do the bare minimum as far as public appearances go and the rest of the time, the two of you hunker down in your hotel room or on the bus.

"Finn, Landon, Miguel and I want the files. All of them. You can't keep trying to do this solo. Send us the information, let us sift through the personnel data and see what we can find. You only have to keep her safe for two more weeks, then we'll all be together again for that last show in Baltimore. If we're lucky, we'll have a suspect. If not, there will be enough of us there to protect her. Okay?"

Fergus had spent the last month feeling very, very alone in his attempts to keep Aubrey safe. He'd been a fool. He had a partner in the security company, and more than that, he had family...a *big* family that would always be there to help him.

"Okay," he said, realizing for the first time just how hard it had always been for him to let go of the control. "I should have asked for help."

Colm reached over and gripped his shoulder in a caring, brotherly way. "You've always been a part of this family, Fergus, but I'm not sure you ever really understood the benefits package."

Fergus laughed. "Only-child syndrome?"

Colm nodded. "I had a twin brother. We loved the same things at the same time. I learned from the cradle what it meant to share my toys, but along with that, I also understood there would always be someone to share the load. We may not be brothers, man, but that doesn't mean I won't do the same for you."

Fergus swallowed heavily, touched by his cousin's gesture, his compassion and understanding. "Thanks, man. For everything."

"We're going to get you through this. And God willing, at the end of it, you'll have that beautiful woman to call your own, to love for the rest of your life..." He paused before adding, "You poor bastard."

Fergus laughed, then he and Colm headed back to the arena. He had a woman to protect...and to love.

11

Aubrey stood on the balcony of her hotel suite, looked out across the Inner Harbor, and sighed.

It had been two weeks since she'd had sex with Fergus...since the stalker had made an attempt on his life.

She'd tried to push him away, but Fergus remained true to the promise he'd made the first day they'd met. He'd stuck to her like glue. Though he had respected her use of the safe word, no longer initiating sex, he'd doubled down on the rest. He never left her side whenever she wasn't on the bus or in a hotel room, though she hadn't done that any more than necessary, too terrified of the prospect that something bad might happen to Fergus.

At night, Fergus also stayed close, sleeping next to her in bed, either on her bus or in her hotel suites. He no longer touched her, no longer kissed her. Just lying next to her, letting her know he was there, that he would keep her safe.

He'd given her the distance she'd asked for emotionally, if not physically.

And it was killing her.

Her insomnia had returned with a vengeance, but with him beside her, she'd been forced to stay in bed, quiet, dreaming of his hands, his lips, his everything.

She also hadn't worked on her music once during the entire past two weeks.

Both of those things made her grumpy, walking around like a dog with a thorn in its paw.

Fergus stepped next to her, clearly enjoying the view more than she was. "There's nothing like Baltimore in the summer. Look at that blue sky. The sun reflecting off the water. And smell that."

Aubrey took a deep breath, failing to catch any scent that she found remotely pleasant. "Garbage? Stagnant water? Pollution?"

Fergus shook his head, though his grin never faded. "Come on, Aubrey. It's time for you to see a part of Baltimore even *you* can't criticize."

"I'm tired, Fergus. I think I'm going to hang out in the hotel today."

The last thing she wanted to do was sit around in yet another nondescript hotel suite, but that seemed imminently safer than going anywhere with Fergus in his hometown. She'd heard too many of his stories over the past six weeks...about his Pop Pop and the pub, his parents, the Inner Harbor, the aquarium, the art museum he loved on North Charles Street. He'd painted a picture of this city she'd found hard to resist.

The town she called home, God help her, was L.A. A city filled with plastic people, traffic, smog, and greed. She hated the city. Hated what she'd become there.

Fergus grasped her hand—it was the first time he'd touched her since Houston—and dragged her toward the door. "You're not hiding one more day, Aubrey."

"You're the one who *told* me to hide."

"And I'm revoking that order. Come on."

She stopped walking and tried to pull her hand away from him, but he tightened his grip.

"You can walk out of here under your own steam, or I'll toss you over my shoulder. Choice is yours."

"Fergus. Wait."

He paused by the door, and she forced herself to look at him —*really* look at him. She'd been avoiding doing so ever since the attempt on his life. Because looking prompted longing, and longing made her whole body ache.

But now she saw there were dark circles under his eyes, stress lines marring his forehead, his shoulders tight, tense.

She'd thought *she* was a wreck, but Fergus beat her. Was it fair of her to ask him to stay inside another day when his family —the people who brought him peace and happiness—were so close?

Perhaps she could convince him to leave her here.

Yeah, right.

"We only have a couple more days. I don't want to push our luck, you know. I mean..." She struggled to find words that would make sense. The lack of sleep was really messing with her. "We've already managed to put some distance between us. Maybe we should just...keep it there. It'll make it easier when it comes time to say goodbye."

Fergus frowned. "No."

"What?"

"There's no distance between us, Aubrey. I want you more now than ever. Don't assume the fact I haven't touched you is a sign I've given up. I've been hired to protect you, and I can't let anything distract me from that. But I've been working on a plan, a way to keep you safe and, God, maybe even trap the stalker. I had to wait until we got here, to Baltimore, because my family is going to help. Right now, they're the only ones I can trust with your life."

"You're in danger too." Every time she closed her eyes, she saw that lighting rig fall, saw Fergus leaping out of the way with only seconds to spare.

"I can take care of myself."

She shook her head. "The stalker doesn't fight fair. Everything's been a sucker punch, something no one ever saw coming. How do you protect yourself from that?"

"By remaining alert—and not letting myself be distracted by how beautiful you are, by how much I want to kiss you, touch you, pull you under me and bury myself deep inside you."

Aubrey was out of fight...on all fronts. "I want you too."

He smiled, and she realized it was the first time he'd done so in two weeks. "Good. Hold on to that thought. Actually, maybe I should prove to you exactly how little distance there is between us."

He pressed her against the nearest wall to give her the kiss of the century. His tongue stroked her lower lip, urging her to open her mouth to let him in for a taste.

Aubrey ran her fingers through his hair, then let them wander toward his face so she could touch his close-trimmed beard. Fergus was taking advantage of the opportunity to explore as well, his hands drifting under her shirt to touch her breasts.

The kiss grew more heated, her arousal reaching critical mass in record time. It had been too long since he'd kissed her, and every second of the time since had been spent waffling between fear and sexual frustration.

Aubrey drew her hand along his chest, making her way to his jeans. She only managed a glancing touch of his very hard, very erect penis trapped beneath the denim, before his hand circled her wrist and pulled it away.

"No. We can't do more than this, Aubrey."

"Yes, we can," she said, trying to break free of his grip, intent on unfastening his jeans and getting a skin-on-skin touch.

"No," he repeated more firmly. "I didn't mean to let that go so far. I lose all control with you. We don't have time to do this right, and I'm not settling for a quickie."

"We don't have to be anywhere until late this afternoon. We have hours."

Fergus chuckled. "One minute you're pushing me away, the next you're dragging me to your bed."

He had a point, though she hated to admit it. "I know. I'm

sorry. I'm really bad at..." She didn't know what word to use to describe what was happening between them.

"Relationships," he supplied. "And I've noticed. But don't worry. I'll teach you."

"Says the man who's never had a long-term girlfriend."

He nodded his head just once as if to say touché. "Then we'll learn together. As soon as this stalker is caught—"

"What if we don't catch him?" It was the question she'd never let herself voice before. The label had hired him to be her bodyguard during the duration of the tour, which ended tomorrow. It would be the height of stupidity to expect the stalker to just fade back into the woodwork, which meant...what? Fergus had a new business to run. He had signed on to guard her because of the short time frame. That time had run out.

"We're going to catch him." Fergus seemed determined not to consider the alternative to that. "And when we do, when the tour is over, you and I are making up for lost time. Tell Blair to clear your schedule for a week. Maybe two."

Aubrey laughed, even as she shook her head. She'd had too much time lately to think about the two of them, and every time she played it out, it ended the same way. With him in Baltimore and her in L.A.

She'd been down this road before, let herself fall in love, dream of a future, and every time, it crashed and burned in spectacular fashion.

"Why are you shaking your head?" he asked.

"Because I don't want to hurt you."

Fergus studied her face for a long, quiet moment. Aubrey fought to hold his gaze and not squirm under the scrutiny. "You still don't get it," he said at last.

"Get what?"

"As soon as the concert is over tomorrow, you're going to be my girlfriend. We're dating—exclusively."

"Have you forgotten we live on opposite coasts?"

He shrugged as if that meant nothing. "Tour's over. That

means you start writing songs for the next album. You can do that anywhere...including Baltimore. Sunnie moved in with Landon shortly after I got back to the States, so there's an empty room in the Collins Dorm we can claim until we find our own place."

Fergus had obviously been thinking about their future together as well. And his looked a lot different than hers. Hell, his even included living arrangements.

Aubrey wasn't sure how to respond to that, but Fergus didn't give her time when he looked at his watch and said, "We gotta go. We're late."

"For what?"

"We have a lunch date we need to get to."

"Where?"

"Pat's Pub. Come on."

He resumed his grip on her hand and this time she didn't resist, didn't fight. They walked through the kitchen of the onsite hotel restaurant to a back door, and there, she discovered a vehicle with dark-tinted windows waiting for them. The driver opened the door, and Fergus quickly ushered her to the back-seat, climbing in to sit next to her.

The drive to the pub was a short one. If she'd been anyone else, they actually could have walked it, but no doubt Fergus didn't fancy the idea of the two of them getting mobbed by fans on the street. The driver pulled up behind the pub. There was a locked back door, but Fergus produced the key and ushered her in.

As soon as she entered, she was assaulted by the smell of baking bread. She sucked in a deep breath of the delicious air. "Now *that's* a good smell," she murmured as they walked down a small hallway, passing a storage closet and the restrooms.

Once they entered the dining room, Aubrey smiled as she looked around. Fergus had described it to her once, declaring the pub his favorite place. She could see why. It wasn't particularly crowded at lunchtime, yet she got a sense the people here were regulars. More than that, they were friends.

There was an older version of Padraig and Colm manning the bar. He waved when he saw them. "We were just wondering where you were."

Fergus led her to the bar. "Uncle Tris, this is Aubrey."

Tris shook her hand. "Nice to meet you."

"And this," Fergus said, gesturing to the old man sitting at a stool in the center of the long mahogany counter, "is Pop Pop."

Aubrey had never truly believed in love at first sight—but one look at the sweet, dear man's face, and she fell. Hard. He smiled kindly, the look accentuating the deep laugh lines by his bright blue eyes. His gray hair was thinning but not completely gone, and though she knew he was in his nineties, she was impressed by how fit, how healthy he looked. She'd bet he had been a lady-killer in his prime.

"It's very nice to meet you, Mr. Collins. I've heard quite a lot about you, and now I see where all the men in the family get their good looks."

"Damn," Fergus muttered. "I've just lost you to my grandfather, haven't I?"

Aubrey laughed and nodded. "I think you might have."

Pop Pop, the rascal, enjoyed the joke, giving her a wink as he laughed as well, the sound truly jovial, infectious.

Aubrey claimed the stool next to the older man. "I hope you'll forgive me if I act as if I know you. Fergus has told me so many wonderful stories about you and your family."

"He gets his storytelling from me."

She nodded. "Oh, no worries there, Mr. Collins, he gave you credit for all those wild Irish tales."

"It's lovely to meet you, lass, but if you *truly* knew me, you'd know that 'Mr. Collins' thing won't fly with me. We're in the pub. And in the pub, I'm Pat. Or Pop Pop, if you prefer."

Aubrey swallowed heavily, wishing she had the gumption to take him up on that offer. The sum total of her family was one—

just her. She'd given up thinking of her mother as anything more than a bad cold she simply couldn't shake. "Pat," she said.

He narrowed his eyes. "No. I've changed my mind on giving you an option. Pat doesn't work either. Not for you. It's going to have to be Pop Pop."

Clearly, Fergus got his take-charge attitude from this man as well as his handsomeness. "Pop Pop," she repeated softly, blushing as she did so.

"I think I see what Finn and Miguel have been going on about these past couple of weeks," Pop Pop continued. "You made quite an impression on the Collins men at the bachelor party."

"It was nice of them to let me tag along."

Aubrey glanced toward the front door of the pub as it opened, smiling when the very men they'd been talking about entered, along with several others.

They walked to the bar, and Aubrey had never felt so tiny in her life. It was as if she were suddenly a fairy who'd been banished to the land of giants.

Miguel, Finn and Landon all said hello, Miguel giving her a quick kiss that earned him a warning growl from Fergus.

"Still possessive of his girl, I see," Miguel muttered.

Aubrey didn't know how to respond to the "his girl" comment. Fergus's family and friends—like Fergus—seemed to think they were a couple. And while Fergus had told her that was what he wanted, she wasn't sure it was fair to let anyone think that was true with so much still up in the air.

"Miguel—" she started, ready to correct the misconception.

Fergus cut her off, introducing her to his uncle Aaron, who was also a cop, and two more very attractive male cousins, Lochlan and Lucas.

"You sure do make big guys in your family," she remarked to Pop Pop.

"Good Irish stock," he declared.

She looked at Fergus. "This is our lunch date? It feels more like a second bachelor party."

He shook his head. "The guys are *my* lunch date. We're going upstairs for a war council, getting our ducks in a row for tomorrow's concert."

"What about me? Shouldn't I be involved in that?"

"I'll fill you in later, I promise. You're already sitting with *your* date, though given the way you're looking at him, I'm not sure I can trust you two alone with each other. I'm afraid Pop Pop will try to steal you away from me. You think Miguel lays the charm on thick…"

Aubrey shrugged playfully. "Oh, believe me, that's a definite possibility. I have a thing for older men," she teased.

"Is that so?" Pop Pop threw in. "Well, then, I make no promises, Fergus. You know I'm a sucker for a pretty singer. Now, if you can cook, my dear…"

Aubrey feigned a wince. "I knew I should have signed up for cooking classes."

They all laughed, and the rest of the men drifted to a doorway near the back of pub that she assumed led to the apartment upstairs. The Collins Dorm, Fergus called it.

Fergus hung back until the others had gone. Standing behind her stool, he wrapped his arm around her, giving her a quick kiss on the top of her head. He wasn't hiding his feelings for her from his family, and his actions felt natural and right after two long weeks of rigid, forced distance.

It was nice to see Fergus in his true environment, acting like himself rather than a bodyguard. She hadn't seen him like this since the night of the bachelor party. While Fergus the Bodyguard was sexy as sin, there was something even more irresistible about Fergus the Family Guy.

"We're just going to be upstairs," he said, more to his uncle Tris and Pop Pop than to her.

"We'll keep her safe," Tris said, with the same confidence

she'd come to understand was a trait all the Collins men possessed.

Then Fergus spun her stool so that she was looking at him. "My mom and dads are stopping by the pub at some point this afternoon to meet you. They have tickets to the concert tomorrow, and I promised to introduce them then, but they couldn't wait. Okay?"

She nodded. "Sure."

"I realize there are a lot of us and it can be sort of overwhelming."

Aubrey shook her head. "Actually, it's not. They're all really nice," she said softly. "I like it here."

Fergus's smile widened, then he gave her a kiss on the cheek and headed to the apartment.

Yvonne, yet another of Fergus's cousins, introduced herself, then asked if they wanted the lunch special. They did. Tris walked around the bar to take the drink orders of a couple who'd just walked in, leaving her alone with Pop Pop.

As they ate, they spoke for a little while about the tour, the cities she'd seen, and how unbearable the heat in Baltimore was in July.

Fergus's parents *did* stop by briefly, the three of them taking a short break from their jobs to come meet her. She'd been charmed by Fergus's fathers, and though initially nervous meeting his mother, Lily, the woman had put her at ease instantly. The three of them promised they'd have more time to visit after the concert, then said their goodbyes.

She had just finished the most incredible fish and chips she'd ever had when Pop Pop turned the conversation to her.

"So, tell me about yourself, Aubrey."

She shrugged. "There's not that much to tell that you probably haven't seen splashed all over the covers of the tabloids."

Pop Pop frowned. "You forget who you're talking to. My daughter is Teagan Collins. I know perfectly well the tabloids never get it right."

"Oh, I don't know. Truth is, the tabloids probably make me sound more interesting. I'm pretty boring in reality."

"I find that hard to believe. Tell me about your family."

Aubrey hated that question. "I...I don't have any. Well, I mean...my mother and I are estranged. She stole a fair amount of my money, and now we're handing over what's left to the lawyers in a bitter lawsuit that's dragged on forever."

Wow. She hadn't meant to offload all that onto the poor kind man. "I'm sorry, Pop Pop. I think that sounded way more bitter than I meant it to."

"I think you're entitled to some bitterness. I apologize for bringing it up. You'll have to forgive this nosy old man."

She smiled. "It's a pretty basic question. You couldn't have known my family tree is actually a cactus. Your family is so nice, so normal."

Pop Pop chuckled. "Stick around a little while and see if you want to continue to use *normal* as a way to describe this crazy tribe. It's nice to see Fergus so happy."

"Isn't he always happy?"

Pop Pop nodded. "Yes, but there are certainly degrees. I know he was pleased to come back home last September, but it took some time for the shadows in his eyes to lift. We've talked a bit about his time overseas. I think he saw some things that shook him, changed him, made him harder. But with you, I see shades of the loving, kind, patient boy who left us to join the Army."

Fergus didn't talk much about his time with the military. Or at least not in any detail. She was glad to know he'd shared with his grandfather. She had learned—through Fergus—that talking about things could be very therapeutic.

She was definitely seeing a shrink when she got back home. It was obvious she couldn't untwist the knots inside her alone.

"Heaven knows I tested that patience. I'm afraid I wasn't very nice to him when he first started working as my bodyguard."

Pop Pop's expression told Aubrey he was aware of that.

"He told you?"

"He called me a couple of nights at the beginning, asked for advice."

"What did you tell him?"

"I told him to listen to your music, to your songs. That's where your truth lies."

"You've listened to my albums?"

Pop Pop nodded. "Finn wasn't the only one with a wee crush on Jenny Sweet. I live with Finn's parents, Aaron and Riley. As such, I was subjected to more of those silly teenybopper sitcoms than I care to admit. I can't say much for the show itself, but it was worth enduring for the ending number each week. That was when your true spirit shone through."

"I don't know what to say. No one's ever realized..."

"It's the same way with my Teagan. She's actually quite shy. It was hard for her to express herself as a child. The music she wrote let her do that. It was the same with my Sunday too. Love at first sight, it was. And while she was the most beautiful woman I'd ever seen, it was the music she sang that set my heart racing."

Pop Pop pointed to a small framed picture hanging behind the bar. "That's her. Tris," he called out. Tris had returned to the bar and was mixing drinks farther down the counter.

"What do you need, Pop?"

"Hand me that photo, son. The one of your mother and me."

Tris grinned as he took the frame from the wall and gave it to his father. Something in Tris's face told her this was a frequent request. Tris returned to making his drinks as Pop Pop handed her the frame.

The photo was black and white, and Aubrey's suspicions were confirmed. Pop Pop in his younger years was every bit as handsome as Fergus.

Then she studied the woman with him. Sunday had long dark hair, and there was no denying she was lovely, but there was something else about her. In the picture, they stood in front of this pub, Pop Pop with his arm around her shoulders as he grinned widely at the camera. Sunday's arms were wrapped around his waist, her face in profile as she looked at him.

The love, the happiness...the *trust* in that gaze took Aubrey's breath away.

"Two fools in love," Pop Pop murmured. "Starting off on a grand adventure. New country, new business. We'd traveled here with precious little, but Sunday never complained, never wanted anything more than me, this ramshackle place and our family."

Aubrey sniffed, dashing away a tear. "Thank you for showing me that."

Pop Pop looked at her, and he—like Fergus—seemed to see all the things no one else ever noticed.

"You've been hurt before."

She nodded, trying to swallow the lump that had formed in her throat. "Yes."

"Your mother?"

"And others."

"Don't let them win. Don't let them break that beautiful spirit of yours. I'm going to make a wish for you, lass."

She smiled sadly, his words bolstering her, yet at the same time, making her want to curl into a ball to cry out a lifetime of pain.

"What wish?" she asked, her voice thick.

"That one day, you're the woman in a photo like this. Standing with the man you love. Stepping into an uncharted future, certain of only one thing—that you'll never want for anything that truly matters because you already have it."

"You ready to go?"

She jumped slightly, turning at the sound of Fergus's voice behind her. Aubrey tried to paste on a casual smile, tried to hide her emotions, but the way Fergus narrowed his eyes told her she hadn't perfected the look.

"Everything okay?"

Aubrey nodded and stood, still holding the picture. She

glanced at it once more. "Don't take this the wrong way," she said to Fergus, finally finding a genuine grin. "But Pop Pop tells the bedtime story better than you."

Fergus laughed, taking the framed photo from her. "He cheated. Used pictures."

Pop Pop gave them a quizzical look, but didn't ask what they were talking about. Instead, he winked at her, then lifted her hand for an old-fashioned kiss. "I'm not sure when I've enjoyed a lunch date more."

Aubrey leaned toward Pop Pop, kissing him on the cheek. "Thank you," she whispered. "For the wish."

"I hope to see you again very soon."

They left the same way they'd entered, the car and driver waiting for them. "Back to the hotel, or should we go on ahead to the arena?" Fergus glanced at his watch. "It's a bit early."

"Let's go to the arena. Maybe we can finish sooner. Room service in my suite tonight?"

Fergus nodded.

Dining alone together had become their norm after the attack on his life. It had been a fairly quiet event each evening, with Fergus, scrolling through the personnel files and reading the data his cousin Finn was putting together with the help of Miguel and Landon. The cops had taken advantage of their access to police records and had run several background checks on various crew members with previous arrests.

So far, Doug was in top contention, even though Aubrey simply couldn't believe it. However, the evidence kept piling up...and it certainly seemed to point to him.

He'd been seen backstage during all the concerts when the "accidents" occurred. Then Miguel discovered that her ex actually had a police record for several arrests, including shoplifting, possession of marijuana, and—the one that had really surprised her—manufacturing an explosive device. That information, paired with his apparent obsession with winning her back by following the concert tour, had made him their prime suspect.

They entered the M&T Bank stadium through a secured entry and found Marcus, who filled her in on the next day's busy schedule. He led them to the club floor. They passed a comfortable lounge on the way to a smaller room that her team would use to do her hair and makeup. They'd just reached the room when Marcus's phone rang.

He looked at the screen, then back at them. "I need to take this. Just hang out here, and I'll come back for you when we're ready for the sound check."

Fergus opened the door, but the two of them hadn't made it more than a couple steps inside when they pulled up short.

"Doug?" Aubrey said, her eyes wide. "*Blair?*"

Blair and Doug were both naked, having sex on the couch.

"What the hell?" Fergus growled.

Blair squealed with shock, reaching for something to cover herself while trying to shove Doug off of her.

Doug stood up but didn't bother with clothes, facing the two of them, his hands shielding his erection. "So, uh, I guess this looks pretty bad."

"It doesn't look good," Fergus muttered. Aubrey wasn't sure, but she thought she detected a slight tone of amusement in his voice. However, she discounted that when she looked at his furrowed brows and angry scowl. Nope, Fergus certainly wasn't entertained.

Blair managed to pull her sundress on, but it was inside out... and backwards. "I'm so sorry, Ms. Summers!" she squeaked, hiding behind Doug.

Fergus glanced down, then bent over to retrieve Doug's cargo shorts, tossing them across the room. "Get dressed."

Doug gave Fergus an appreciative smile as he casually pulled on the shorts. "Thanks, dude."

"You're the one who's been letting Doug in backstage," Aubrey said flatly to Blair, who was peeking around his shoulder, her face beet red, her eyes shifting everywhere to avoid looking at her.

Blair nodded, clearly miserable. "We didn't mean for it to happen, but we just…"

"We fell in love," Doug said. "This beautiful angel found me right after you and me had that talk, Fergus. The one where you said I didn't have a chance at getting Aubrey back. I was low, man. Lower than low. Blair found me and…well, there's just no stopping it, dude. It's chemistry. It's love."

Aubrey smirked as she listened to him. When they'd first met, he'd sworn it was true love as well. She'd been inexperienced enough—and depressed enough—to soak up his words at the time.

Now she could see the truth. Doug was a harmless, goofy puppy dog, who fell in love as easily as most people changed clothes.

"So you haven't been following the tour to win Aubrey back?"

Doug shook his head as he wrapped his arm around Blair. "It's been wicked hard for the two of us to find time and, er, places to, um, express our, well, you know. To…visit."

Visit was obviously synonymous for fuck in this instance.

"Whenever I had a free afternoon," Blair said, taking up the explanation, "I'd find somewhere private for us to meet up. Then I'd sneak him back out again before the show started."

Given the level of intelligence the two lovers possessed, Aubrey was actually shocked they'd managed to hide their affair as long as they did.

"You have an arrest record," Fergus said.

Doug seemed surprised that Fergus knew about that. Or maybe he was confused about why it mattered. "Yeah. Did some stupid shit when I got out of high school. Couldn't find a job, didn't have much money. I stole a burrito from a convenience store. Got busted and the cops found the joint in my pocket."

"What about the explosive device?" Fergus asked.

Doug laughed. "Oh man. That was *really* stupid. Me and a couple buddies got stoned one night and decided we were going to make fireworks. My one friend, Kyle, looked up how to do it on the internet. We seriously didn't expect the thing to work, but it did. Made one hell of a fucking boom. Burned Kyle's eyebrows off. Dude looked funny as shit. Anyway, a neighbor thought we had a bomb. He called the cops and we spent the night in jail."

Fergus sighed as all his evidence was discounted. "Blair, you knew we suspected Doug of being the stalker. Why didn't you step forward to explain? Do you know how much time we've wasted investigating the wrong man?"

Blair lowered her head, a sure sign she was about to cry. Aubrey rubbed her eyes. She hated it when Blair cried.

"Oh, hey, man," Doug said. "We're real sorry about that. I told her I didn't think she should tell anyone about us. I didn't want to hurt you again, Aubrey."

Doug had apologized to her at least a million times since Christmas, but she'd never once accepted it, never believed he was truly sorry for his actions.

This time...she did.

"It's okay, Doug," she said. "I'm happy for the two of you. Honestly."

Doug grinned widely. "Thanks." Then he turned to Fergus. "Treat our girl good, Ferg. Aubrey's one in a million."

Fergus nodded, though Aubrey could feel the tension growing in him. She, like him, had allowed the lack of any further attacks and the building evidence against Doug convince them they were on the right track.

Or maybe they'd latched on to him because he seemed like a less dangerous foe.

Now they were flying blind again.

Doug shrugged on his shirt and the two of them picked up their shoes.

"We'll talk about this next week, Blair, when I'm back in L.A.," Aubrey said.

"Yes, ma'am."

The two lovers looked at Fergus, waiting to be dismissed.

"We're done here." He picked up his walkie-talkie, requesting a security guard report to the dressing room. Once the guard arrived, Fergus asked the man to escort Blair and Doug out of the stadium.

"Dammit," Fergus said, when they were alone again.

"Fergus, even with all the evidence, you knew Doug was a long shot. This guy, this stalker, is dangerous and he's..."

"Still out there. Get one of your backup singers to do the sound check. We're going back to the hotel."

Aubrey texted Marcus, who agreed to let Janice fill in for her. She was just about to put her cell away when it rang.

She sighed when she saw the number on the screen. "My lawyer. Hello?" she said, answering it.

"Aubrey. It's Ross. Listen. I just got off the phone with your mom's lawyer. We've reached a settlement. One I think you'll be pleased with."

"Really?"

"She's agreed to pay back the two million she stole to invest in her own fashion company."

"And the contracts?" Her mother had signed contracts on Aubrey's behalf until she'd turned eighteen. At that point, she'd still trusted her mom, so she had signed the next one herself—without realizing she'd been giving the lion's share of her earnings from the show *and* the royalties from the first four albums to the hateful woman.

Of course, at the time, she and her mother shared a lawyer, and her mom had been fucking him. God, hindsight really was twenty/twenty.

"She'll renegotiate them. The fact is, she did manage you, so she's still asking for a percentage of future earnings on the show and those first albums, but it's a much more reasonable share."

"And the punitive damages?" Aubrey had tacked on a large number, one she knew her mother, in all likelihood, couldn't afford. It was a petty way to strike back, but that old adage was true. Hell hath no fury like a woman scorned...three times.

"She has offered half."

Aubrey knew her mom. Knew there was a catch. "What's the condition?"

Ross hesitated long enough that Aubrey realized she was right. "She wants to speak to you in person."

Aubrey hadn't lain eyes on her mother since finding her in her bed with Doug. She'd sworn then she'd never let the woman get near her again.

"Aubrey," Ross said. "You still there?"

"I'm here. I need to think about it. I'll get back to you."

"We have a chance to settle this now...and out of court. It's just one visit."

"I'll let you know." Aubrey hung up the phone.

Fergus looked at her. "Your mom?"

She nodded. "When it rains, it pours."

He pulled her toward him, offering the warmest hug in history. Aubrey was starting to get spoiled by them. Anytime the bottom fell out, he was there, wrapping her up in his strong arms, making her feel safe and...

God, she couldn't recall the last time she'd felt genuinely lonely.

Even with the distance between them the past two weeks, she'd never felt alone because he was there, close, and if she'd asked him for help, for anything, he would have given it to her.

"Want to talk about it?"

She shook her head. "No. Not really. Can we go back to the hotel?"

He nodded. "Sure."

"And can we go to bed? Together? Preferably naked?"

"Probably. Safe word?"

"I'm taking it back," she said.

He laughed. "Then definitely."

12

Fergus stood outside Aubrey's dressing room, arms crossed, as he listened to the voices through his earpiece. The security detail for this venue was off the charts, countless guards in position all around the stadium.

In addition, his uncle Aaron had pulled in every favor, stationing uniformed and plain-clothed cops at both ends of this hallway, and then every twenty feet or so along the path he and Aubrey would take to the stage.

Hunter had wrapped up his performance, and the crew was working their magic, swiftly switching from Hunter's stage set to hers. Marcus had just given him the three-minute warning, which meant it was time for he and Aubrey to start making their way to the stage.

While he loved watching her perform, Fergus would rather be anywhere else at the moment than here, with sixty-thousand screaming fans. Because somewhere out there was a man determined to hurt Aubrey.

He knocked on the door. "Aubrey. It's time."

She opened the door and he smiled, offering her a wolf whistle, hoping it would wipe away her visible nervousness.

She rolled her eyes and smiled. "You've seen every costume countless times."

"Doesn't mean you're not hot every time you wear them."

"We can hear you," Miguel said through the earpiece. *"Tuck your dick back in and focus."*

Fergus chuckled, gesturing to the mic clipped to his shirt collar to clue her in that other ears were listening. "Microphone."

She laughed. "Let me guess. Miguel is jealous."

Miguel answered, even though Aubrey couldn't hear. *"Remind her I think she'd made a terrible mistake picking you over me."*

"Gentlemen," Aaron said, jumping into the conversation. *"Can we keep the chatter to a minimum? Are you on the move yet, Fergus?"*

"We are now."

He wrapped his arm around Aubrey, and the two of them began what felt like the longest walk he'd ever taken. He noticed the undercover cops standing guard as he passed them.

They entered the field beneath a long tent that kept Aubrey hidden as she approached the stage. There was a tall flight of stairs there that she would climb. Her entrance to the stage would start from thirty feet up, and she'd slowly descend another staircase on the other side as the music started.

He followed her nearly to the top of the covered rear stairs, both of them remaining out of view until she was introduced. The roar of the crowd was deafening when it became apparent Aubrey was about to appear.

"I'll be waiting on the side of the stage," he said, raising his voice to be heard. "Exit stage right."

Aubrey nodded. "Okay," she said, though he read the words on her lips, the sound drowned out by the first strains of music.

He squeezed her hand, and Aubrey leaned toward him, giving him a quick kiss on the cheek before wiping away the lipstick left behind with her fingers.

He forced a smile. He was terrified, but he couldn't let her see. He'd move heaven and earth to keep her safe. That was all she needed to know.

Aubrey climbed the last few stairs alone, and if he'd thought the cheering had been loud before, he'd just been proved wrong as the stadium erupted.

"I don't have eyes on her," he said, hoping someone, anyone, could hear him over the din.

He quickly descended the stairs, taking up his position on the right side of the stage.

Miguel, who was standing on the other side, gave him a thumbs-up. Glancing toward the back of the stage he could just barely see Landon standing behind a large speaker, guarding the rear.

On a regular night, under normal circumstances, Fergus would have considered this one of the best nights of his life. He was standing backstage at a rock concert on the Baltimore Ravens field. This was the stuff teenage dreams were made of.

Especially when Aubrey broke from her usual set to sing a song she promised would be on her next album.

Fergus had heard bits and pieces of "Haunted Dreams," but he didn't realize she'd finished it. Then she confessed that while she'd shared the music with her band, they'd never performed it together, not even in practice.

Fergus stood spellbound as she started singing. The song shared the dreams of two young lovers. The first verse was about a man, so far from home, fighting in a war he didn't understand. The second was about the woman he'd left behind, alone and lost in a room that held nothing without him there.

She looked at him as she sang the chorus the last time.

Time stood still for just a moment as her gaze met his.

He was looking at his future. His forever.

He smiled, and she returned it before turning back to the crowd. The thunderous applause as she finished the song proved she had another hit, maybe the biggest of her career yet.

Two hours later, he heard the familiar opening to her signature song. Glancing across the stage, he saw Miguel talking to Erick as he took his place, ready to fire the cannons. Tonight's show was a little different because there were six additional pyrotechnicians at the rear of the stage, in position to set off a fireworks display the second Aubrey's song ended.

"Okay," Aaron said in the earpiece. "Fire in the sky time. Everyone on alert."

They'd all agreed that if the stalker was going to strike, the most dangerous times were prior to the show or at the end. The noise of the fireworks was going to make it difficult for them to communicate with each other, so keeping Aubrey surrounded the moment she exited the stage was vital. Landon and Miguel both gave him the thumbs-up.

Once the song ended, they were going to make their way toward him.

"I'm here." Finn touched his shoulder. He'd been stationed in front of the stage, but was part of the team escorting her back to the dressing room. "Aaron's on his way."

Fergus glanced at his cousin and nodded. So far, so good.

He recalled Aubrey's comment about the stalker's attacks being sucker punches. He scanned the area, searching for anything that might be amiss. Everything seemed to be going as planned.

Which meant he was missing something.

Something was about to happen. Fergus could feel it. Even Aubrey did. Twice she'd glanced his way, and he wasn't sure, but he thought he could detect a slight quiver in her voice.

He gave her a comforting smile, and his brave woman powered through it, the song building, her voice growing louder, stronger, as she reached the final high note.

Fergus looked back across the stage, hoping to catch Miguel's eye, to see if he shared this same feeling of dread. Miguel was doing the same constant scan he'd been conducting. Then the cannons started to fire.

He glanced toward the board, surprised to find Erick had

been replaced by someone Fergus didn't know. He could only assume the head pyrotechnician—a role he'd assumed after Dave's injury—had joined the team firing off the fireworks.

Aubrey's last note hovered in the air, and then the dark night was awash in color as the first of the fireworks lit up the night sky.

Fergus watched the first one flash, then took a step toward the stage, hand outstretched for Aubrey.

She turned toward him, and smiled as the crowd screamed and cheered, and a thousand cameras flashed in her direction. She gave them one last wave and then...

She disappeared.

Fergus watched in horror as the stage opened up and Aubrey fell through.

He pulled his gun from the holster beneath his jacket and ran toward the opening, aware from the cheers that the crowd thought her disappearance was part of the act.

The opening had been created for Hunter's grand entrance, the trapdoor rigged mechanically so that he could be raised up slowly from beneath the stage, appearing through the effects of the fog machines and special lighting.

The fireworks continued to light up the sky, a constant cacophony of sound.

"I've lost her!" he screamed, racing to the opening and diving through, just before the trapdoor closed once more.

It was strangely quieter under the stage. Not completely quiet, but the loud booms of the fireworks were muted.

"Tell your men to stay back."

Fergus squinted in the near darkness, looking toward where the voice had come from. The stadium lights had been dimmed to allow viewers to enjoy the spectacle of the Fourth of July display. He could make out two figures, but he couldn't see their faces. They were just silhouettes, more shadow than form.

"Tell them!" the man shouted again.

"Everyone hold your positions," Fergus said.

Aaron's voice was frantic as he said, "You have her? You have her?!"

"Negative."

"That's enough. Take off the microphone, crush it with your foot."

Fergus didn't want to give up his only means of communication, his only way to get help.

"Do it *now*."

He pulled the mic off, crushing it with his boot.

"And the earpiece."

Fergus took it out as well, tossing it next to the useless mic.

The man's voice was familiar, but Fergus struggled to place it.

"Aubrey? Are you okay? Are you hurt?" Fergus asked.

"I'm fine," she said, her voice trembling. "He has a bomb, Fergus. It's strapped to him."

Fuck.

"Who?" he said.

"Erick," she answered. "It's Erick!"

Now he understood why he couldn't place the voice. Though the sound was right, there was no stutter.

"Erick," Fergus started. He still had the gun in his hand. Either Erick hadn't seen it or—perhaps more alarming—he didn't care.

The area beneath the stage began to lighten and the fireworks stopped, even though they should have continued for quite a bit longer. Aaron must have thrown up the alert. The stadium lights would already be flooding the field, every spotlight used for the concert turned up full force. As such, the area beneath the stage grew a bit brighter, though it was still dim.

Now, instead of shadows, he could see Erick and Aubrey.

What he saw made him wish for darkness again.

Erick was wearing a vest of explosives, the detonator in one hand, while his other arm was wrapped around Aubrey's throat, holding her in place before him.

She was breathing rapidly, her face pale, her eyes wide with fear.

"It's okay, Aubrey," Fergus murmured.

The light revealed his weapon, but Erick didn't demand that he drop it. He probably believed Fergus wouldn't fire it.

Fergus understood that assurance. If his shot missed, he'd hit Aubrey or the bomb. God only knew if that would set the thing off—and Fergus was hoping to never find out.

The front and both sides of the stage were solid wood, built to keep anyone in the crowd from slipping beneath.

The only way to get where they were standing was through a curtained area at the rear, where most of the light was coming from. Erick had wisely placed his back against one of the solid pillars holding the stage in place, blocking any shot from that direction.

The footsteps that had been racing across the stage faded away, proving Aaron had cleared it.

Given the number of explosives on Erick's vest, Fergus hoped Aaron was able to clear the stadium quickly. If Erick fired that detonator, he wouldn't just take out the three of them. He had enough explosives strapped to him to take out a fair chunk of the stadium. Thousands of people would die in the blast.

The light was just bright enough to reveal the detonator the man held wasn't a dead man's switch. That was probably the only damn thing Fergus could be grateful for at the moment.

"What do you want, Erick?" Fergus asked in a calm voice, praying he could find some way to talk the man out of this suicide/murder/terrorist attack of his. And if not, Fergus needed to stall, to give the police a chance to formulate and enact a plan that would save them all or, barring that, give him an opening to take the shot.

"I wanted *her*."

"Then you can have me," Aubrey said, her voice still quivering.

"Aubrey," Fergus warned.

"I'm right here," she said, determined to draw Erick's attention away from Fergus. "No one has to get hurt. Let's just leave together."

"I made flames for you, Jenny. Sweet flames."

Fergus tried to come to grips with that. Erick had actually become a pyrotechnician to impress her? He'd only begun acting on his obsession during this tour...but it was clear his unhealthy infatuation had started a long time ago.

Erick tightened his grip around her, but given the bulkiness of the explosives strapped to his chest, it was an awkward hold.

"We're *going* to be together, Jenny. It just won't be in this world. You fucked that up when you fucked *him*! You didn't need him. You had *me*. I was protecting you, taking care of those guys who hurt you!"

"I see that now," she said. "I'm sorry I didn't before. It's not too la—"

Her word was cut short when he tightened his grip, her hands flying to her neck. Erick was cutting off her air.

"She can't breathe," Fergus said as she continued to struggle.

Erick didn't seem to realize how tight his grip was. He loosened his hold, his arm moving lower, then his hand slipped into her dress, engulfing one of her breasts. "How does it feel, Fergus? To see your slut in the arms of another man?"

Aubrey's eyes closed tightly, and Fergus could see how hard she fought not to cry.

"You were mine, Jenny. *Mine*!"

Erick looked at Aubrey and saw Jenny Sweet, saw the girl from the show, the one he—like so many other young boys— dreamed of marrying one day.

"Please, Erick," she said.

Hearing her speak his name seemed to spark the very thing Fergus dreaded to see in the man. Determination. Erick was resolved, ready to die.

His thumb twitched.

God. Time was up.

"Aubrey," Fergus called out quickly. "Trust me." It was a tall order, but they were out of time. "Relax—*now*!"

Mercifully, she understood.

She went limp as Fergus lifted the gun.

Her suddenly dead weight caught Erick unaware. The man tried to hold her up, even as the thumb of his other hand moved to the switch.

Fergus fired, the bullet piercing Erick just above his right eye.

Aubrey crawled away rapidly as Fergus raced forward. The detonator hit the ground a second before Erick's body did the same.

The sound of the gunshot prompted the police to action, and Fergus realized they'd gathered quietly on the other side of the curtain, waiting for their opportunity.

Aaron grasped Fergus, taking the gun from him, pushing him away from Erick's body. "The bomb squad is on their way. Get Aubrey and get the hell out of here."

Miguel and Landon were helping Aubrey to her feet. She was trembling uncontrollably when he reached for her.

"Aubrey!"

She fell into his arms, sobbing. He held her for just a moment, then half-carried, half-dragged her from beneath the stage. "We have to get out of here."

She made a weak attempt at walking, but whatever strength had kept her going when Erick held her captive was gone. Fergus stopped and bent to pick her up, carrying her as she clung to his shoulders.

"I was so scared," she whispered.

"I know, Butterfly. I know. It's okay now. I've got you." He carried her back through the tent, though part of it had fallen—or the cops had torn it. The police had done an amazing job moving people out of the stadium, most of the seats empty already. They ran into Marcus in the hallway. He was yelling orders into this phone, but hung up when he saw them.

"Thank God you're okay, Aubrey!" he exclaimed. "The police said there was a bomb."

Fergus nodded.

"This way." Marcus led them down a secluded hallway to an exit not used by the public. A car was waiting there, the driver hopping out and racing around to open the back door for them. Fergus helped Aubrey in, climbing in with her.

"To the hotel?" the driver asked.

Fergus shook his head. "No. Pat's Pub." Too many members of his family had been at that concert watching the show, and he wouldn't rest easy until he saw each and every one of them with his own eyes and knew they were safe. "I need to know my parents and the rest of my family got out of the stadium. That they made it home."

Aubrey lifted her head and gave him a small smile. "They'll be okay."

"I know," he said, praying that was true. He'd left his uncle Aaron, Miguel, Landon and Finn back at the field with the bomb. "Even so, there are too many of them still there with that bomb. Sunnie will kill me if anything happens to Landon."

He rubbed his eyes wearily, too many faces flashing before his eyes. He hadn't fired a gun at another man since his time in Afghanistan. "Erick," he started, stopping when he realized he didn't have a clue what he wanted to say, how he could ever verbalize his feelings.

"Fergus." She cupped his face, her eyes searching his. "You're remembering something, aren't you? From your time in the Middle East."

He nodded. "Erick's not the first man I've killed."

She wiped her face, trying to dry the tears that hadn't stopped yet. "I'm sorry. Sorry you had to do it again for me."

He pressed his cheek against the top of her head, holding her close, breathing in the smell of her. Every emotion crashing down on his head—fear, relief, regret, hope, anger, happiness.

The only thing keeping him grounded right now was having her here in his arms, safe, alive.

They rode in silence the entire way to the pub. As they got close, he instructed the driver to pull up in the back.

They unlocked the back door and he led her into the pub. As he'd expected, they had closed the pub, the only people gathered there his family.

His *whole* family. Even those who hadn't been at the concert.

Like him, they were all worried, so they'd come here to wait together.

"You closed the pub," he said, drawing everyone's attention to them.

"This is closed?"

If he'd been in a better state of mind, he might have laughed at Aubrey's question. The place was more crowded now than it was during a lunch rush.

His mom cried out his name when she saw him, racing across the room to hug him. "Fergus! The news..."

He glanced at the television and saw the stadium, a "Breaking News" banner along the bottom.

"They said there was a bomber at the stadium."

"There was," Fergus said. "He's dead."

Dad stepped next to his mother, reaching out to grip his shoulder, the strength in that touch fortifying him.

"Aubrey," Mom said, after releasing him, turning to hug her tightly. "We were so worried about you!"

Fergus caught the brief glimpse of surprise on her face as his mother said exactly what a normal mom would in the face of such horrors.

Aubrey lifted her arms, returning the hug, the tears she'd only just managed to stem flowing freely again. His mom, bless her, let Aubrey hold on for as long as she needed, offering her words of comfort until she was able to pull herself back together.

Daddy placed a strong arm around her shoulders, guiding her to a table in the center of the bar. Fergus followed, and they sat down with Pop Pop, telling everyone what had happened and answering their questions. Hunter and Ailis had arrived at the pub just before them, so they'd already known that Aubrey had been taken, and that Fergus had been with her under the stage. Apparently, that was all they'd learned before Marcus had insisted they leave.

Fergus noticed that Sunnie's gaze never left the television. He knew she wouldn't rest until they knew the bomb was defused and Landon, her dad, and her brother were safe.

They all continued to wait, talking and fretting quietly as they watched the news. And then, about an hour later, Aaron called Riley to tell her they were all on their way back to the pub.

After that, the entire atmosphere changed as Tris and Padraig started handing out the pints of Guinness, everyone slowly relaxing as the reality sank in that everyone they loved was safe.

Cheers erupted when Miguel, Aaron, Landon and Finn arrived a few minutes later, and they filled in the rest of the blanks. The bomb was defused—according to Aaron, there had been enough C4 to blow up half the stadium—and Erick's body had been removed.

The police in Erick's hometown had immediately been dispatched to his apartment, where they'd discovered one entire room decorated with photos of Aubrey as Jenny Sweet, and even more explosives. His opportunity to act on his obsession had appeared when he'd found a job posting for a pyrotechnician position, traveling as part of Aubrey's crew.

As the night wore on, they shook off the fears, the conversations turning to more normal, less terrifying things.

Aubrey spent the better part of half an hour talking to Teagan about her songwriting, and Fergus was happy to see the horror of the night slowly fading as she spoke to her idol. He smiled when Teagan commented on "Haunted Dreams," and Aubrey told her Fergus had inspired it.

Though it was well after three in the morning, and they had a wedding the next day, no one seemed ready to part. It was Sunnie—normally the life of every party—who put her foot down.

"I have planned a stellar wedding reception, and I'm not going to abide one single yawn from any of you," she called out. "Go home. Now. All of you."

Fortunately, Sunnie had planned an evening wedding.

"Back to the hotel?" Fergus asked as everyone started making their way either to their cars or upstairs.

She glanced up. "Do you think I could see this dorm of yours?"

He grinned. "Definitely."

Sunnie had eschewed the tradition of the groom seeing the bride before the wedding. After the night's scare, she refused to spend the night away from Landon, and the two had left, hand in hand, to return to their apartment.

Fergus took her upstairs. Finn and Colm were kicked back on the couch, though it was apparent they didn't plan to stay there for long. Yvonne was standing at the kitchen counter, drinking a bottle of water.

He held out his hands. "And these are my roommates."

Aubrey laughed. "I hope you guys don't mind if I crash here tonight."

Yvonne smiled. "You can stay as long as you want."

Finn cleared his throat, his grin wide. "I don't mind sharing *our* room with Aubrey, Fergus."

Fergus rolled his eyes. "We're taking Sunnie's old room."

"Party pooper," he muttered as he and Colm stood and walked to the stairs.

"Good night," Colm said.

Yvonne said her good nights as well, heading to her room.

Fergus took Aubrey's hand, leading her down the hallway. "You might be sorry you asked to stay here. The bed in her room is full-size, not nearly as big as the king in the hotel suite."

"It'll be big enough for what I have in mind."

Fergus closed the door as they entered, locking it behind them. He kissed her, the fears and stress of the last few hours pouring out of him. He held her tight, never wanting to let her go.

He'd almost lost her.

The reality of that shook him.

"Aubrey, I..."

She cupped his cheek. "However you need it."

He unzipped her dress, both of them realizing at the same moment that she was still in her final costume, a low-cut sequined dress that was far too glamorous for Pat's Pub.

She giggled softly as the shimmery material fell to the floor.

"Go lie on the bed."

She did as he asked, lifting her arms to him once he'd shed his clothing as well. Fergus climbed over her, caging her beneath him.

They'd slept together last night, coming together in a rush. Two weeks of celibacy had taken its toll on both of them. It had been fast and furious and afterwards, exhaustion caught up with them. After too many restless nights, they'd both managed a decent night's sleep.

Tonight, he felt a different sort of urgency.

Aubrey hadn't agreed to take him up on his offer, to stay with him in Baltimore while she wrote her next album. He'd told her he wanted to date her. In truth, what he wanted was so much more, but he didn't dare tell her that.

The concepts of trust and love still frightened her. Simply asking to date her was as far as he'd ventured to push.

For now.

But Fergus knew he wouldn't be able to hide the depth of his feelings for long. Maybe not even through tonight.

He kissed her again, taking the time to savor the moment. Every day since he'd met her, there'd been some unknown threat lurking in the wings.

"He's gone," Aubrey whispered. "I forgot what it felt like to not be afraid."

"I know." He kissed her again. "When you fell through the stage...Aubrey...I thought—"

She lifted her head, kissing away his fears. "I don't want to talk about it. Erick has stolen enough from us. Tonight..."

"Is ours."

He ran his fingers along her slit. Aubrey was hot, wet, ready.

Fergus had always approached sex as a game, playing to win, just as he would in football or chess. It had never been that way with her.

But tonight was even more different. He wanted to make love to her. To show her everything she meant to him.

Those three little words hovered right on the tip of his tongue. Every time they started to escape, he kissed her.

Placing his cock at her opening, he slid in slowly, their lips still joined, their tongues dancing together.

He lifted his hips languidly, over and over, taking her slowly, deeply.

Love you.

The words kept slipping into his subconscious, begging to be spoken.

"Aubrey," he whispered when he sensed she was close.

Before he could verbalize his feelings, she fell into the abyss, her back arching, her eyes closing.

"Yes!" she cried out. "Fergus. My Fergus."

Her declaration, her claiming, pushed him over as well, and he came inside her, filling her.

When he lay down next to her, she curled into his arms, falling asleep within moments.

It figures, he thought with a grin. The second he was ready to declare his undying love, the insomniac found sleep.

Tomorrow.

He would tell her how he felt tomorrow.

13

Aubrey laughed as Fergus spun her around on the dance floor. She'd never been to a wedding like Sunnie and Landon's in her life. The entire event was a pop culture fan's dream. Apparently Sunnie, who'd known Landon since they were just kids, had decided to document their lives together through a flashback of all the things they'd loved.

The entire waitstaff was dressed in their Disney finest. The waitresses had donned their princess attire, every single heroine embodied, including her favorite, Mulan, while the waiters represented nearly every Prince Charming, from Aladdin to the Beast.

The song ended and Fergus led her back to their table, where several family members were sitting, eating cake, drinking and chatting.

Aubrey grinned when something on the far wall caught her eye.

There were four screens, one on each of the walls of the ballroom, each showing different videos—all on mute.

One screen displayed old family videos, where Aubrey was getting yet another peek of Fergus as a boy.

"It's you again," she said, pointing at the screen.

Fergus rolled his eyes. In the video, he, Landon and Finn were wrestling in Riley and Aaron's living room, at what Lily claimed was a birthday sleepover gone wrong.

"Riley let them eat all the candy from the piñata. Before dinner," Lily said, shaking her head.

"Not one of my finer parenting moments," Riley said, though her grin made it clear she thought it was funny now. "They were hyped up on sugar. Wild beasts. It was sort of scary at one point."

The three boys couldn't have been more than eight or nine, and they were clearly out of control. Riley and Aaron looked haggard in the video, but in the background, it was easy to see Pop Pop egging them on.

"You were a lot of help, Pop," Riley said sarcastically.

"Promised a dime to the winner," Pop Pop said, chortling with laughter as he watched the old video.

"By the way," Fergus said. "You still owe me that dime."

Pop Pop shook his head and pointed to the screen. Landon had taken an elbow to the eye, and Sunnie could be seen comforting him, giving him a hug. "I gave Landon the dime just before the wedding service. Figured he came out on top in the end, winning the heart of our sweet Sunnie."

The family videos had already looped through twice, but Aubrey struggled to look away, enthralled by every single minute.

A second screen flashed music videos from Sunnie and Landon's middle and high school years. Everyone got a kick out of looking back at the hairstyles and fashions that had been popular a decade or so earlier.

"Hey, Aubrey," Miguel called out, pointing to the screen.

Aubrey was surprised to find *herself* as part of the montage on the third screen, where Sunnie was showing highlights from all their favorite TV shows growing up.

She'd chosen to show the scene Miguel had reenacted the first time they'd met. It was funny how Miguel had managed to change her impression of that scene. She hadn't watched a single episode of *Sweet Flames* since leaving the show six years earlier. Her first boyfriend, Brett, who played Prince Alexander, was there on his knee, declaring his undying love to Jenny Sweet.

She would have expected to feel some pain over seeing it again, but instead, all she could remember was Miguel, doing his impersonation of the prince and making her laugh at the cheesiness of it all.

The final screen featured just one thing, looping over and over.

It was the viral video of Sunnie and Landon, recorded just after he'd saved her from a mugger, kissed her, and the two of them realized they were meant to be.

Aubrey had actually seen the video when it first went viral, though she hadn't realized until nearly the end of the bachelor party that Landon was the "hot cop" and Sunnie the "saved nurse."

"I'm stealing this beauty for a dance," Miguel announced, drawing Aubrey out of her seat.

"Just one," Fergus said. "I'm not about to spend tonight like I did the bachelor party, watching you and Finn dance every song with my girl."

Fergus looked at her, using that stern face that sent her mind straight to the dominant man she hadn't spent nearly enough time with in the bedroom. She hoped to broaden her sexual horizons tonight after the wedding.

She'd managed two whole nights of sleep—both eight hours straight. She couldn't believe how clear and bright and wonderful the world looked after a restful night...and some amazing sex.

"Save all the slow dances for me," Fergus demanded.

She shook her head. "I'm afraid you're going to have to find another partner for one of them." Aubrey gestured toward Pop Pop.

"A young man's folly," Pop Pop said. "As we older, wiser men can tell you, you have to ask for those slow dances at the beginning of the night."

Fergus laughed. "Pop Pop, you gotta stop hitting on my girlfriend."

Everyone at the table laughed as Miguel led her to the dance floor, the two of them joining a circle of Fergus's cousins.

Aubrey couldn't remember a more magical night.

She never wanted it to end.

F̲ERGUS GRINNED AS HE SKIRTED THE DANCE FLOOR AND caught a glimpse of Aubrey's face. She looked well-rested, at ease, happier than he'd ever seen her.

He left the ballroom and walked down the hallway, looking for the men's room. It was a good thing they were taking an Uber home. He'd had three bourbon and Cokes, and he was in the mood to celebrate—not only the wedding, but love and life. It was hard to believe that last night, he and Aubrey had come close to losing theirs at the hands of a madman.

The memory of it kept sneaking up on him, sucker punching him. He figured it would take time—a lot of it—before he fully shook the fear of almost losing her in such a violent way.

"Excuse me," a female voice said.

Fergus stopped and smiled at the stranger. The wedding reception was being held in a hotel ballroom. He assumed this woman was one of the guests of the hotel, as he didn't recognize her. "Yes?"

"I wonder if I can impose on you to help me. It's rather embarrassing."

"I'll help if I can."

The woman gestured to the floor. It took Fergus a moment to realize that the woman's heel had gotten stuck in one of the heating grates. The hotel was an old one, recently refurbished. The architects who'd remodeled it worked hard to keep a lot of the original design to maintain the historic look.

"I'd take the shoe off but, well, as you can see, it's not the most practical design. And there's nothing here to hold on to.

I've nearly fallen twice already. I was about to start yelling for help when you appeared."

Fergus laughed as he knelt in front of her. The shoe was one of those types that laced around the ankle. He'd never understand the fashion behind women's shoes.

He gently gripped the shoe, trying to unwedge it without damaging it, but the thing was lodged tight.

The woman wobbled, grabbing on to his shoulders for support.

Fergus wiggled it again, the woman gripping him tighter.

"Please take pity on me and tell me you weren't the groom."

She was flirting with him.

"I'm one of the groomsmen." And then, just to cut her off at the pass, he added, "I'm here with my girlfriend."

"Lucky woman," she purred, one of her hands slipping beneath his tux jacket.

She'd attempted to make it look like an accident, but Fergus could tell the difference. Then he realized the reason he was struggling was because she wasn't helping. In fact, she seemed to be working against him, putting weight on the shoe every time he nearly freed her.

Enough of this.

He started to stand. "I think you're really stuck. I'll go grab someone from the reception des—"

"Oh no, please," she said, holding him down. "I think you've nearly got it."

Fergus gave the shoe one more hard tug, not bothering to be gentle this time.

Her shoe slipped free.

He stood back up, stepping away from her. Her hands fell to her sides.

Fergus nodded politely, ready to extract himself from the woman. "Well, then, if you'll exc—"

"I can see why she's attracted to you. You're very handsome.

Have you ever considered modeling? Or maybe acting? I could help you with that."

Fergus frowned, confused. "I'm sorry. Do we know each other?"

Before she could respond, there was a gasp from behind him. He recognized it well. He'd heard it several times over the past six weeks.

"Aubrey," he said, turning toward her, alarmed by her pale complexion. "What's wrong?"

Aubrey wasn't looking at him. Instead, her gaze was locked on the woman next to him.

"What are you doing here, Mom?"

Fergus jerked, this time spinning to face the woman who'd made Aubrey's life a living hell.

Like her daughter, Candace wasn't looking at him, but smiling smugly at Aubrey.

"Hello, my dear. You never responded to my settlement offer, then I heard about the stalker and the bomb. I came to make sure you were all right."

Aubrey shook her head. "No. That's not why you're here."

Candace laughed. "Always so suspicious. Can't you just accept that as your mother I might be concerned? You were nearly blown to bits after all. It was on every news station last night. Your picture...on every channel. I called in a favor of a dear friend and flew here on his private jet."

Aubrey appeared tense, but he couldn't hear any trace of anxiety in her tone. "No. I can't accept the idea that you might give a shit."

Fergus couldn't either. There wasn't a spark of worry in Candace's face. If anything, it felt more like she viewed the horror of last night's events as some stellar publicity stunt.

"How did you find me here?"

"Marcus."

"Why would he tell you..." Aubrey sighed. "You played the devastated mother card."

Candace laughed. "My tears are quite irresistible. He said you were fine and that you'd spent the night at Fergus's family's pub. After that, it only took a few Google searches. When I saw the sign of the pub's door, explaining it was closed for a family wedding, it was simple enough to follow the trail here. I must say, your taste in men is improving."

Candace took a step closer to him, attempting to place her hand on his arm. Fergus withdrew it with a scowl.

Aubrey's mother shook off his retreat. "Your handsome body-guard was helping me out." She gestured toward the grate. "My shoe got stuck."

"Right," Aubrey said, sarcastically.

"This is a private party." Fergus hated that Candace had the power to ruin what had been an amazing night just a few minutes earlier. "I'm going to have to ask you to leave."

Candace smiled. "I've booked a room in the hotel."

"Then go there." Fergus started toward Aubrey, but Candace reached out and grasped his arm.

He was amazed by the nerve of her. "You have two seconds to move your hand."

Rather than respond to the genuine threat in his tone, Candace smiled, though she did release him. "Oh, Aubrey. You've definitely bitten off more than you can chew with this one." She looked back at him, staring at him as if he was a steak and she a starving wolf. "If you ever want a real woman in your bed," she murmured softly.

Aubrey had once described her mother as beautiful, the type of woman to draw a man's eye, to make him want her. Fergus saw none of that. Everything about Candace was fake—from her hair color to her heavily made-up face to her so-called motherly concern. Once again, he thought of his mom and how much she cared about him. He hated that Aubrey had never felt that pure, unshakable, unending love.

"You know, there was always some part of me that hoped, even after everything Aubrey said, that you'd somehow redeem yourself. That you'd realize how special, how wonderful your daughter is. But I can see now that's never going to happen. You're selfish to the core."

Candace narrowed her eyes briefly, just long enough to let him know he'd struck a chord. "You're wrong. *She's* the selfish one. She'd be *nothing* without me—and every now and then, she needs to be reminded of that fact. Don't you, dear?"

Fergus's jaw clenched with anger.

"No. I don't."

He turned, surprised to see Aubrey walking toward them. She didn't stop until she was standing directly next to him. "Why are you here?"

"I thought...it's high time we put this lawsuit nastiness behind us. You know you don't want to sue me. I'm your mother."

Aubrey laughed, though there was no humor in the sound. "You know you've lost. You can't win when our case goes to court. That's why you offered the settlement with that condition. What did you think would happen? I'd see you with Fergus and fall apart?"

"Your demands in that settlement are ridiculous. You wouldn't be anything without me, Aubrey. It's time you stop pretending you know what you're doing, time to drop the suit. I was very good for your career and I can be again. You must see that."

"Are you insane?" Fergus started, but he stopped when Aubrey placed a hand on his arm.

"I see things very clearly actually. I recognize all the ways you put me down throughout my life, always insisting it wasn't my talent that got me where I was, that it was your skill as a manager. And you worked very hard to make sure that I never got close enough to anyone who might build up my self-esteem, who might open my eyes to your game."

"I brought you to L.A. I opened those doors for you," Candace said, her anger palpable.

"I was three years old, *Mom*," Aubrey said bitter, drawing out *Mom* as if to prove it meant nothing to her. "And the only door you opened was the one to your bedroom."

Candace's hand was up and flying through the air in a flash. Fergus was quicker. He caught her wrist before her slap connected with Aubrey's face.

Fergus had never been more furious in his life. "Don't you ever raise a hand to her again. I promise you, you won't like the results."

"That's my boy," Dad said.

Fergus's gaze shifted toward the entrance to the ballroom. His parents and Pop Pop were standing there. From the dark looks they were shooting in Candace's direction, it was obvious they'd been there long enough to hear what was happening.

"Good catch, son," Daddy added.

Fergus might have laughed if he weren't still tense, still holding onto her mother's arm.

"Here's how this is going to play out," Fergus said to Candace. "You're going to crawl back into your hole—but before you do that, you're going to sign that settlement agreement and give your daughter back the money you stole from her. If her lawyer can't make that happen, you can be damn sure the ones in *my* family will. And then, you're never going to speak to her again."

Candace tugged her arm away from him, her eyes narrowed in anger. "You're just the bodyguard, and while you may think you can control her, can steal her money, I can assure you that I won't stand by idly and allow that to happen. You have no say in her life or—"

"Actually, he does," Aubrey said. "They all do."

His family had moved closer.

Pop Pop placed a protective arm around Aubrey's shoulders. "She has a new family now."

"Yeah, right," Candace snorted. "You can act all high and mighty, but I'm not buying it. You see what's she's worth." She looked at Aubrey. "You're a fool if you fall for this. They'll all have their hands out soon enough, ready to steal whatever they can get from you."

"No. The only one who does that is you."

Aubrey had told him once that everyone was out to take her money. He could see now where she'd gotten that idea from.

"Aubrey," her mother said. "Don't you see? You aren't like other women. You're talented and rich, a star. You can't trust anyone. If I've learned anything in my life, it's that men are users, plain and simple. I know I shouldn't have taken advantage of you when you were younger. I'm willing to make that contract right. I just...I want to be a part of your life again."

Aubrey frowned. "A part of my life?"

"It'll be just you and me. We can own the world."

Fergus recalled all the things Aubrey had told him about Candace. About Aubrey's father kicking them out before she was born. About all the men she'd slept with to advance Aubrey's career. About how her mother slept with all of Aubrey's boyfriends. Listening to her now, it felt as if she genuinely believed everything she was saying, that she was determined to be the only person in Aubrey's life.

"You'll never share the cash cow," Aubrey murmured. "Will you?"

Candace scowled. "What are you talking about?"

Aubrey looked at Pop Pop, who still had his arm wrapped around her. She smiled at him. "I've found something here you'll never understand."

"Aubrey—"

Aubrey raised her hand. "There was only one condition tied to that settlement. That we see each other. Mission accomplished. I'm calling Ross to tell him I've fulfilled my end of the bargain. Sign the agreement or prepare for court. Either way, this —this—relationship," she said, though it was clear Aubrey didn't want to use that strong a term, "is over."

"I'm always going to be your mother. The only one you'll ever have," Candace said, somewhat desperately.

Fergus smiled when his mother moved into their circle, reaching for Aubrey's hand. "Not the only one," Mom said.

Aubrey glanced appreciatively at his mother, tears filling her eyes. He read the words *thank you* on her lips, aware that Aubrey was too touched to speak.

"I don't...you can't..." Candace was sputtering, trying to understand. It occurred to Fergus Aubrey's mother had never seen this side of her, never fully comprehended how strong her daughter was.

"Goodbye, Candace," Aubrey said. Fergus had never heard a more final farewell in his life.

And apparently neither had her mother. Candace stared at her daughter, her arrogance dimmed. She was speechless for several moments before walking away without saying anything else.

"Are you alright, my dear?" Pop Pop asked.

Aubrey nodded. "You know, I spent the entire day soaking up what it felt like to be a part of your family, of being a Collins. The whole time, I kept waiting for someone to pull the rug out from under me."

Fergus reached for her, but she shook her head.

"No one is going to do that. I won't let them."

Mom tugged on Aubrey's hand and gave her a sweet, motherly kiss on the cheek. "I'm so proud of you, of the way you stood up to her. I'm sure it wasn't easy."

"Actually, it was. Because you were all standing here with me."

Fergus smiled. He'd lived a lifetime with his family at his back. He'd never had to consider what it would be like not to have them there. Seeing what it meant to Aubrey made him fully appreciate something he'd always taken for granted.

"I think we should leave these two alone to chat," Pop Pop said to Fergus's parents.

The four of them returned to the ballroom, leaving Fergus alone with Aubrey.

"So...that was your mother," he joked after a quiet, awkward moment of silence.

For the first time since she'd shown up in the hallway, Aubrey laughed, the color returning to her too-pale cheeks. "That was her. Quite a gem, right?"

"Are you okay?" he asked, sobering up.

Aubrey nodded. "I have to admit, when I first saw you standing here, talking to her...for a split second..."

He narrowed his eyes. "Aubrey, I would never—"

"Betray me," she said, cutting him off. "I know that. Know it as well as I know my own name. I trust you, Fergus. Trust you with my life—the one you saved last night. But more than that, I trust you with my heart."

Fergus had held back his feelings for weeks, giving her time to get comfortable with him, with them. He couldn't do it anymore. "I love you."

The tears that had gathered in her lashes finally fell and she sniffled and smiled. "I love you too. I'll never doubt you again. Not even for a second. Although I'm not sure I can make the same promise about doubting myself. I'm kind of a train wreck, in case you haven't noticed."

Fergus laughed. "I can deal with a train wreck. As long as you can handle the fact that I'm a control freak."

Aubrey stepped into his arms. "I have absolutely *no* problem with that," she said suggestively, her hands reaching under his tux jacket so that she could run her fingers over his chest. Fergus cursed his shirt.

"We're wearing too many clothes," he grumbled.

"Society sort of frowns on public nudity."

"Then society is really going to have an issue with this." Fergus took her in his arms and kissed her, long and hard and deep.

When they parted, she placed her hand on his cheek, her fingers stroking his beard. "Take me home?"

He wrapped his arm around her shoulders. "I like the sound of that. Home."

As Fergus walked her back to the ballroom, ready to grab her purse and shawl and offer their goodbyes, his feet never touched the ground.

He was walking on air.

Colm muttered something about the Collins curse claiming another sucker, prompting Kelli, a close friend of the family, to punch him in the arm.

Everyone laughed, but Fergus was too distracted by Aubrey—her smile, her beauty, her genuine happiness.

Nothing could touch him in this moment. He was so fucking grateful that she was here, safe, alive.

His.

$\maltese$ 14 $\maltese$

Aubrey had barely made it two steps into the hotel suite before Fergus picked her up and carried her to the bed.

Rather than take her back to the pub, they'd decided they needed privacy. So, they were taking advantage of her suite.

She laughed when he tossed her onto the mattress. Pulling her heels off, she tossed them across the room.

Fergus watched her with hungry eyes. Very hungry eyes. He took a step toward the bed, and there was no misreading his intent.

Rising to her knees, she narrowed her eyes and put her hands on her hips. "Not so fast, bodyguard. Where's my foreplay?"

Fergus grinned briefly before adopting that stern, sexy, dominant look that made her panties wet. "Oh, it's foreplay, you want, huh?"

Aubrey knew right then and there, she'd screwed up. "Wait."

He shook his head. "No. No waiting."

"Fergus," she started again.

"From this point on, there's only one word that will stop me. Do you want to say it?"

She shook her head quickly, giggling. "Are you crazy? Hell no."

Aubrey thought perhaps he was fighting the desire to smile, but she couldn't be sure. The man had an amazing poker face.

"Turn around."

She did as he said, feeling his weight dip the mattress when he planted one knee behind her to unzip her dress. Fergus tugged it over her head, then made short work of her bra. He snapped the elastic on her thong—with surprising ease—and just like that, she was naked.

Aubrey shivered when he ran the tip of one finger along her spine, starting at the nape of her neck and ending just above her ass, before journeying back up again.

"Fergus," she whispered.

"Shhh. Foreplay."

He stroked her back over and over, each time adding something else to the mix—be it a soft kiss to the side of her neck, or the lightest of slaps on her bare ass.

He spent a good fifteen minutes just touching, kissing and caressing her back.

She started to turn twice, but both times, he held her in place, facing away from him, threatening—if he could call it that —to spank her if she moved.

Aubrey had never had so much attention paid to just that one area of her body.

Finally, mercifully, he told her to lie down on her back.

If she'd thought that meant the end, she had another think coming.

Fergus shifted lower on the bed, picking up one of her feet, massaging it as she moaned in sheer bliss. Then he repeated the same glorious kneading to her other foot. He was seducing her in slow, tantalizing, driving-her-out-of-her-mind degrees.

Next his hands slid to her calves, rubbing firmly, as every drop of tension in her body just fell away.

She giggled when he placed soft kisses on her knees. "Fergus," she whispered.

He lifted his head. "Foreplay," he whispered back, giving her the wink of a scoundrel. He knew exactly what he was doing to her.

Because every comforting touch was provoking two different sensations—complete relaxation layered with painful need. She started to squirm, trying to press her legs closed to still the empty clenching of her pussy.

Fergus was wedged between and not giving way as he dragged the tips of his fingers up and down her thighs, inching closer to the place she needed him most without ever getting there.

When the need grew too much, she reached for the spot herself. It was a move Fergus had been waiting for. From the smug smile on his face, she could tell he'd set her up.

"Tsk tsk," he said, shaking his head as if disappointed.

He moved off the bed, his sudden departure catching her unaware. The bed was colder without him in it.

When he rifled through her luggage, pulling out a scarf, she decided to poke the bear and perhaps buy herself three seconds of relief.

She ran her fingers along her slit, rapidly rubbing her clit as her eyes closed. "God," she murmured.

That was all she managed before he was back on the bed, on his hands and knees above her, her wrists captured in his very strong grip.

Fergus made short work of her bondage. It wasn't like she was fighting him. She'd been in his cuffs just once and loved the feeling.

Tonight, he was taking it a step further. He secured her wrists together with the scarf, then tied it to a slat at the center of the headboard.

"One night, I'm going to tie you spread eagle—ankles and wrists—while I go down on you, make you come on my mouth, over and over. But tonight, I feel the need for variety. I'm going to want access to every part of you."

"Wow," she mouthed. Fergus was the master of dirty talk.

And she loved it. She felt the strong urge to put everything he just said to music.

He returned to the spot between her legs, resuming his stroking of her thighs. For a moment, she thought perhaps they were finally getting to the good stuff.

She should have known better.

For the next thirty minutes, Fergus drove her slowly out of her mind, kissing her stomach, caressing her sides, licking long, wet lines from just above her pussy, through the valley of her breasts to her neck. Then he spent a good fifteen minutes on her breasts, alternating between sucking and nipping at her tight nipples.

By the time he stood up and started to take off his tux, Aubrey felt feverish, her body aching with unslaked needs. She took advantage of his departure from between her legs to squeeze them together, shimmying almost, as she sought her climax.

Through all the foreplay, he'd failed to touch the part that needed him most. Aubrey suspected he could blow on her clit at this point and she'd go off like a bottle rocket.

She licked her lips when his pants hit the ground. Damn. She wasn't the only one hot and ready to go. Her gaze was glued to his cock.

He growled, and her eyes flew to his face.

"What—"

Before she could ask what was wrong, he bent and untied the scarf from the headboard. Her hands were still bound together and he took advantage of that, using the scarf to pull her up and over to the edge of the mattress.

He stroked her lips with his thumb, silently urging her to open up. She had a split second to smile before he gripped his cock and guided it to her mouth.

Now that she had the use of her hands—even though they were bound—she was able to touch him, grasping the root of his cock as she took the head, and then more, between her lips.

Fergus's hands threaded through her hair, his fists closing, holding it, pulling it as he moved her mouth—forward and back —on his dick.

"God, Aubrey. Yeah. Butterfly. So good…"

Aubrey hummed with pleasure. As much as she wanted him inside her, hearing his groans and words of praise made her just as hot.

She tightened her grip on the base of his cock, moving faster, taking him deeper, all at his urging as his hands drove the pace. When she felt certain he was there, close to coming, he pushed her away.

"Ferg—"

Once again, her words were cut short as he bent down to kiss her hard. With strong hands, he half-lifted, half-scooted her back to the middle of the bed. She lifted her arms, wrapping her bound hands around his neck as they continued to kiss.

Fergus came over her, his body radiating heat. It rolled off him in waves and warmed not only her skin, but scorched a trail inside her that led straight to her pussy.

She needed him. Now.

When he chuckled, then tsked, she realized she'd made that demand out loud. She closed her eyes, part wince, part prayer. If he sought to teach her another lesson for trying to take control, she'd expire on the spot.

Fergus gentled the kiss, pulling away to look at her. "I had intended to torture you for a little while with the butt plug and vibrator I saw in your bag when I was rummaging for the scarf."

As delicious as that sounded, she craved something much simpler. "Please," she whispered, before realizing that he might take that request wrong.

She started to clarify, but he kissed her once more. Just a quick, hard meeting of the lips.

"Next time. I can't even share you with a toy tonight," he murmured, and Aubrey felt tears fill her eyes when he placed the head of his cock at her opening.

"Yes," she hissed. "God. Yes."

He thrust in without preamble or caution. One hard, rough shove forward and he was there, buried deep, filling her.

Of course, she was there too. Aubrey cried out loudly as she came, her back arched, her eyes clenched shut as everything inside her exploded bright white.

Fergus didn't give her time to recover. Through her orgasm, he kept moving—retreat, return, retreat, return—each thrust harder, deeper.

Aubrey felt as if she were adrift in a stormy ocean, the waves and wind pummeling her, tossing her about. She was out of control, captive to the elements.

The orgasm simply kept going, and she struggled to figure out if it was the longest climax in history, or a million little ones, each coming on the heels of the one previous.

Her bound hands had fallen from him, resting on the pillow above her head.

Surrender.

Again.

Then, a hundred years later, Fergus was there, lost in the midst of that same sea, tumbling beneath the waves with her as he came. Her name on his lips as he filled her.

He made her want so much she'd never considered before— home, family, forever.

Fergus fell to her side, reaching up to untie her hands before pulling her against him, soft lips kissing her forehead.

They lay together quietly for a few moments, both lost in their thoughts, and nearly asleep.

Last night, Aubrey had faced the devil, terrified there wouldn't be a tomorrow. Tonight, she felt as if the skies had opened and shown her heaven.

She giggled softly.

"Something funny?" Fergus asked, his voice husky, deep. She knew it was based on exhaustion, but damn if her foolish body didn't respond in a way neither of them had the strength for.

"When Erick grabbed me, and I saw the explosives, I thought we were going to go up in flames...and it terrified me. Tonight, we did. And all I want is to do it again. And again."

Fergus tightened his grip on her, chuckling. "Why do I get the feeling a song is coming?"

Aubrey gasped, pushing up the second he said it, the faint tinkling of a melody playing in her mind. She hummed a little bit of it while turning toward the nightstand, where she'd seen a pen and notepad placed there by the hotel.

She quickly scribbled down a few words, though she knew there was no chance this song would escape her. It was already written on her heart.

"What are you writing?" he murmured.

Aubrey hadn't mastered the ability to look at Fergus and not feel her heart skip a beat. He was handsome and so fucking sexy. Tonight, naked, in their bed, she could barely look away from his charming, dimpled grin.

"'July Flames'. The heat, the explosion, the fire, the passion, then cool waves. The lyrics will seem to describe the month, but when the refrain hits, it'll be clear it's a love song," she said. "A sexy one," she added, putting down the notepad to return to his side.

They kissed for a few moments.

Then Fergus pulled away an inch or so and smiled. "I like it. Aubrey, I'm ready to burn again."

EPILOGUE

"Well, now. This is a nice surprise indeed." Pop Pop smiled as Fergus and Aubrey walked into the small living area/bedroom Riley and Aaron had added on to their house when his kids started to worry too much about him living alone in the apartment above the pub.

Fergus hadn't been in the room since his return from the military, which was well over a year ago now. He'd never needed to make the journey here, able to share a pint with his grandfather in the pub a few times a week.

The security business had taken off, thanks in large part to his new fame as Aubrey's bodyguard and boyfriend.

The day after Sunnie's wedding, they'd moved into the Collins Dorm. Though he'd offered countless times to go apartment hunting with her, Aubrey continued to refuse, too enthralled by what it meant to live in a home with a real family. She, Yvonne and Sunnie had become thick as thieves, the three of them indulging in weekly "girls' nights," and Colm and Finn had given her a taste of what it meant to have overprotective brothers whenever fans overstepped.

"What brings the two of you here today?" Pop Pop asked when he noticed Aubrey had her guitar with her. It was actually the reason they'd come. "Are the two of you on the way to something?" Pop Pop gestured to her instrument.

"Nope. Just here. Aubrey finished the last song for her new album," Fergus explained.

"I'd like to play it for you, Pop Pop," she said, opening the case.

Pop Pop smiled widely. "I can't think of anything I'd like more. My own private concert."

Aubrey pulled the chair out from the desk, while he and Pop Pop claimed the comfortable, overstuffed armchairs. Fergus hadn't spent a lot of time here, in his grandfather's living space, but there was no denying the man had made it cozy and welcoming.

Aubrey tuned her guitar briefly, then glanced at them when she was ready. Fergus had already heard the song a couple of times, but he knew that wasn't going to keep the lump in his throat from forming when she strummed the first few bars.

"It's called 'Song for Sunday'," she said.

Pop Pop's eyes softened as he glanced in Fergus's direction.

Shit. Forget the lump. Fergus would be lucky not to cry.

Aubrey had put Pop Pop and Sunday's love to music. Fergus had watched her wrestle with the tune and lyrics for months, determined this song, her gift to his grandfather, would be perfect. In the end, she'd created the most incredible blend of Irish ballad and contemporary music, while the lyrics were a poem that spoke of a love that couldn't be destroyed, not even by death.

When she finished, she looked up shyly. Fergus still marveled over the fact she didn't truly realize how talented she was.

Pop Pop sat still for a moment, then he pulled a hankie out of his back pocket and cleared his throat, overcome with emotion. "Thank you, lass. That was the most beautiful song I've ever heard." His voice was thick with tears he didn't bother to hide, allowing them to flow, even as he smiled. "Yes," he said after a few minutes. "That was a most rare and special gift. I'll cherish it forever, sweet girl."

Aubrey sniffled as she reached for a tissue, wiping her eyes as well.

"It's good that you've come by. I was hoping to show the two of you something."

Pop Pop stood, directing them to one side of the room, as he explained to Aubrey, "This is my family wall."

Fergus grinned. "I forgot about this. I haven't seen it in years. You've got quite a lot of new pictures up here." He looked at Aubrey to explain. "Everyone in our family is represented with a photo, but they've changed as we've grown older."

"The old photos are tucked behind the new ones," Pop Pop added. "I'll admit some of those things are getting a bit thick. I worry about the frames holding all of them."

Fergus followed the direction of his Pop Pop's finger, reaching to take Aubrey's hand when he saw what this grandfather wanted to show them.

"I thought the two of you might be interested in my newest."

"Look at that, Aubrey," Fergus said, smiling. "You made the wall."

Fergus heard Aubrey gasp, and he was confused when she said, "The wish. It came true!"

Pop Pop nodded. "It did indeed."

"Wish?" Fergus asked.

New tears fell as Aubrey looked at Fergus. "The day I met your Pop Pop, he made a wish for me."

"That she would one day look upon her true love the way your grandma Sunday was looking at me in that picture that hangs behind the bar."

Fergus's gaze returned to the photo, studying it more closely. It had been snapped at Sunnie's wedding just after the ceremony, before dinner had been served. The two of them were standing by their table at the reception. He'd seen the photographer, but she hadn't.

He was flashing the camera a grin, his arm wrapped around her shoulders, while Aubrey looked up at him...with so much love and affection, it took his breath away.

Fergus gave her a soft kiss. "We both won big on that wish."

Pop Pop chuckled, then Aubrey turned back to the wall, asking questions about the other photographs.

For the next hour, Pop Pop told her all the love stories reflected in the photographs. Fergus, who'd been away too long, learned some of the details he'd missed while he was away. About Lucas trying to steal the pub from them, about Padraig and Mia's trip to Paris, about how Lochlan didn't want to hire May—the woman who'd obliterated his card-carrying bachelor status—as his PA at first.

The sun had set when they started gathering their things to go.

"You know," Aubrey said to Fergus. "Your Pop Pop really does tell the best bedtime stories."

Fergus shook his head, pointing to the wall. "He cheated again. Pictures."

"Ah, lass, don't be too hard on the lad. He's still young. Of course, if you ever tire of his second-rate stories..." Pop Pop gave him the wink of a scoundrel.

"Pop Pop," Fergus said, crossing his arms, his attempt at looking stern failing as his grin broke free. "You really need to stop trying to steal my girl."

I HOPE YOU ENJOYED THIS FIRST BOOK IN THE WILDER IRISH series. Why not dive all the way in? The next book, Wild Spirit, is available now.

HAVE YOU READ THE ENTIRE WILDER IRISH SERIES? ALL THE books are standalone, so they can be read in any order. Be sure to check out all of them!

Wild Passion
Wild Desire
Wild Devotion
Wild at Heart
Wild Temptation
Wild Kisses
Wild Fire
Wild Spirit
Wild Side
Wild Night
Wild Embrace
Wild Dreams
Wild Chance

FANS OF WILD IRISH AND FACEBOOK! THERE'S A GROUP FOR you. Come join the Wild Irish Facebook group for sneak peaks, cover reveals, contests and more! Join now.

BE SURE TO JOIN MY NEWSLETTER FOR A FREE WILDER IRISH short story, One Wild Night.

TURN THE PAGE TO READ THE FIRST CHAPTER OF <u>WILD SPIRIT</u>, available now.

WILD SPIRIT

"Hey, hey, good lookin'. Whatcha got cookin'?" Yvonne crooned as Leo Watson walked in the back door to the kitchen in Sunday's Side, her family's restaurant.

Leo gave her a half-hearted grin as he placed a large box of produce on the counter. He handed Aunt Riley the delivery list and an invoice. "You got everything except the beans. They're slow coming in, thanks to all this damn rain."

"That's okay." Riley peered into the box. "Damn. Look at those tomatoes. Gorgeous. I have no idea what you Watson boys do to grow such beautiful tomatoes. I swear I think you've got magical powers you're hiding from the world."

Leo didn't even crack a smile. "I wish."

His subdued tone captured Yvonne's attention. Leo had been delivering produce from his family's organic farm since graduating from high school and entering the farming business full time. He and his brother, Josh, worked with their dad, who had farmed the same land with *his* father, while his mother and sister ran the farm market. Back in the days when it had been her grandmother Sunday running the restaurant, the deliveries were made by Leo's grandfather.

Leo came by twice a week with fresh vegetables, and he

typically hung out for a little while to shoot the breeze with her and Riley, or popped over to the pub to say hey to Padraig. For a few months last year, she and Leo had even taken up running together a couple mornings a week because Yvonne had wanted to lose weight, and she'd coerced him into joining her because, while he was totally fit, she'd thought it would help him manage his stress. The jogging club hadn't lasted long, both of them excellent at coming up with excuses not to run.

Yvonne had noticed he'd been a bit of a bear for the past month or two, not saying more than a few words before rushing out again. She was starting to miss him.

"What's wrong, Grumpy Gus?" she asked, pressing her shoulder into his, trying to provoke at least some sort of smile. "You doing okay?"

Leo's frown was firmly in place, as he merely nodded in response.

"You know, I was thinking," Yvonne said, starting to worry about him. Leo was always pleasant, polite, and when she managed to get him to sit still for three minutes, he was funny, great company.

Not that she'd convinced him to indulge in too many of those rare relaxing moments since they'd both left high school and started their own careers. Leo was—plain and simple—a workaholic. And while she didn't find that particularly healthy, he'd always been pretty good at juggling all the balls, so she tried to accept it as part of his nature.

"Thinking about what?" he prompted, clearly intent on heading out without even taking a minute or two to visit like he usually did.

"When was the last time you hung out at the pub with a bunch of us? I know Lochlan, Colm and Padraig would love to see you and catch up. I swear it's been at least a year since we've had the whole gang together."

"That April Fools party," Leo responded.

His answer took her aback. Had it really been that long? "Seriously? That was nearly a year and a half ago."

"I don't have a lot of free time right now, Yvonne. I was lucky I managed to make it that night."

"Make some time," she suggested. "If you don't mind me saying, you look worn out. A night with the Collins clan can cure a lot of ills. Why don't you stop by tonight after—"

"Tonight won't work."

"Why not?"

Leo sighed. "Listen, Yvonne. I need to finish up these rounds and get back to the farm. We're shorthanded and there're a bunch of crops that need to be harvested."

"You're always shorthanded," she grumbled.

"Maybe some other time, okay?"

Before she could reply or even say goodbye, Leo was already out the back door.

"Damn," Riley said, sliding next to her. "That boy is headed for a breakdown."

"He's thirty-one, Riley. Hardly a boy."

Riley shot her a look. "That's not the point. Leo looks stretched about as thin as a body can get. I'm starting to worry about him."

Yvonne nodded, turning when the timer went off to pull the large pan of shepherd's pie out of the oven. She'd been helping her aunt cook in the restaurant since middle school. She loved to cook, loved spending time here in the midst of all the delicious smells, reworking old recipes that had been passed down from Grandma Sunday to Riley, and now to her.

This restaurant was her happy place, her Mecca, her dream job. Sunday's Side was connected through a large open doorway to Pat's Pub, the business her Pop Pop had been running ever since he'd arrived in America from Ireland.

Her dad, Ewan, managed the restaurant with her aunt Keira, and Yvonne's plan for the future included cooking in the kitchen and eventually taking over the running of Sunday's Side, after

Dad and Keira retired. Her cousin, Padraig, planned to assume the helm on the pub side and was already sharing the tasks associated with running it with his father, Tris.

Yvonne had known pretty early on exactly what she wanted to do with her life, so from a career standpoint, she'd always had her shit together. It was everything else she couldn't seem to get a handle on.

"I'm worried too," Yvonne confessed. "But what can we do? You know Leo. He's a private guy and he's not the type to complain. If he doesn't want to tell me what's going on, I'm not sure how to help."

Riley shook her head. "If the mountain won't come to Muhammad, Muhammad must go to the mountain."

"Meaning?"

Riley rolled her eyes. "Seriously? I need to explain this to you? After all the years you've spent in this kitchen with me while you were growing up? Something I figure your poor mom regrets allowing."

Yvonne laughed. Her mom adored Aunt Riley, she honestly and truly did. But the women were as dissimilar as salt and sugar. Riley was loud, flamboyant, opinionated and had a tendency to pepper her sentences liberally with the "F" word. The first time Yvonne let that whopper slip, her mom had pointed at her dad and said, "I blame Riley for this."

Dad had promised to ask Riley to clean up the language around Yvonne and she could attest to her aunt's efforts to do so. Riley's cursing turning to flavorful "near misses" as she turned fuck to fudge, shit to sugar and bitch to biscuit. However, she abandoned that game when Yvonne turned fifteen because "it was too fucking exhausting." After that, she'd let the language fly, then followed every curse word with "Don't say that in front of Natalie or she'll kick my ass."

And Yvonne had managed to follow that rule...mostly. At least until after high school.

"Meaning," Riley said, shaking her head in disbelief over having to explain herself, "you know better than to listen when people feed you a line of bullshit. Listen with your eyes, not your ears. He says he's fine, which is a bold-faced lie. You saw him. I'm pretty sure he was wearing that same shirt the last time he was here—and it hasn't been washed. The damn thing is filthy. His hair is shaggy, which is unusual for him. He's long overdue for a haircut...and a shave. He never comes in here looking all scruffy-faced like that. There are darker circles under the dark circles under his eyes, and if he's slept more than five hours a night this past week, I'll eat my bra."

"You're wearing one today?" Yvonne joked.

"Smartass," Riley said, chuckling. "That boy needs an intervention."

Yvonne considered that as Riley walked over to begin mixing the dough for the homemade bread they planned to serve with the special tonight.

Yvonne began to unpack the box of produce, putting the vegetables away as she recalled the first time she'd seen Leo look so done in.

It had been the night of graduation. Lochlan's parents had planned a blowout celebration for him and several of his closest friends, and Yvonne had been headed to her car, planning to drive to the party, when she'd noticed Leo sitting alone in the school parking lot...

YVONNE GLANCED AROUND THE QUICKLY EMPTYING PARKING lot. Most of the graduates and their families had already shared the hugs, taken the requisite seventy-two million cap and gown pictures, and headed out.

She tucked her keys back in her skirt pocket and walked over to him. "Leo?"

Though the window was rolled down, Leo didn't look up at the sound of her voice. He didn't even seem to see her approaching his truck.

She thought he looked far too depressed for someone who had just graduated from high school. If it was her who'd just busted out of this joint, she'd be dancing naked in the streets right about now. She walked right up to the driver's side window of his pickup and said his name again.

He raised his eyes, meeting hers slowly. There was utter devastation on his face.

Something that wasn't a complete surprise. He'd been subdued and...well, sad, for the past few weeks. She and Lochlan had both asked him if he was okay, had tried to cajole him out of his misery, but nothing had worked. Leo would simply tell them he was fine or offer some lame excuse for his melancholy— blaming it on nerves over graduation or stress over end-of-the-year exams.

Neither she nor her cousin truly believed his reasons, but Leo wasn't ready to tell them what was really wrong, so they'd given him space and time.

"What happened?" Yvonne asked.

He blinked a couple of times, and she wondered if he'd heard her. He was looking at her with a faraway expression.

"Leo?"

This time, her voice penetrated. He leaned back against the driver's seat, his shoulders slumped. "Oh. Hey, Yvonne."

"Everyone else is heading over to Uncle Will and Aunt Keira's house for the party. Are you coming?"

He shrugged, then shook his head. "I don't feel much like celebrating."

Yvonne hated seeing him like this, and she was tired of tiptoeing around him. Avoiding problems wasn't her style, so she crossed in front of the truck, opened the passenger door and slid in.

"Yvonne," he started, clearly intent on feeding her the same line of bullshit he had the past few weeks in an attempt to get rid of her.

"I'm not getting out of this truck until you tell me what's wrong," she insisted.

He scowled. "Nothing's wrong."

"Liar."

Leo crossed his arms, stubbornness setting in. She smirked. She could out-stubborn a mule. If he wanted to go a round or two, she was game.

She crossed her own arms, mimicking his annoyance and his posture.

When she held his gaze, he gave in a little. "I've just got some stuff on my mind. Things I need to work out on my own."

"Like what?"

"What part of *on my own* confused you?"

Yvonne narrowed her eyes. "Acting like an asshole won't budge me because I know you're not a jerk. So I'll repeat the part that clearly confused *you*. I'm not getting out of this truck until you tell me what's wrong with you."

"You'll miss the party." It was a lame last-ditch attempt. He was running out of ammo.

"I don't care. It's not like I graduated. I still have to endure another year of high school hell." She didn't really mean that. Truth was, she enjoyed most parts of high school, though she didn't think she'd like it as much next year without Leo and Lochlan there. She was going to have to find a new group to eat lunch with, and that sucked.

"Seriously, Yvonne. I made a mess of something, and I have to figure out how to fix it on my own. This isn't something you can—"

As he spoke, something in the center console caught her eye. "What's that?" she interrupted, pointing to a small ring box.

Leo quickly picked up the box and put it in his pocket. He clearly hadn't meant for her to see it. "Nothing."

"Is that an engagement ring?"

There was no way Leo would propose to Denise. For one thing, they were way too young. And for another, Yvonne had gotten the impression the couple was on the verge of breaking up. Something she and Lochlan had mused was probably what was bothering Leo.

He and Denise had dated ever since the Homecoming dance their sophomore year. They'd been called the "perfect" couple by everyone at school—except *her*, though she'd given up her crush on him at the beginning of this year when it was obvious Leo still only had eyes for Denise. Yvonne had gone out with a few guys since then and was currently dating Ricky Bernard.

"Deo"—the ridiculous couple name Lochlan had given Denise and Leo—were even crowned king and queen at this year's junior/senior prom.

"Are you insane?" Yvonne asked, when it became apparent that was indeed what was in the box. "You can't propose to Denise."

"I already did." Leo turned away from her, looking toward the school.

"What? Why would you do that? Tell her it was a mistake. You're only eighteen, Leo. What would possess you to—"

"She's pregnant."

Yvonne fell silent, her stomach clenching in panic. No wonder he'd been so quiet lately, so worried. "What are you going to do?"

"I'd planned to take responsibility for my actions. I was going to make things right."

"That's not still the plan?"

"She turned me down. Said she wouldn't marry me."

Yvonne frowned. "Why would she do that?"

"She said two wrongs don't make a right. That she wasn't going to make this whole situation worse by marrying me."

"But..." Yvonne was flabbergasted. "You two have been a couple for nearly three years. Why would she have stayed with you that long if she didn't love you?" Yvonne had never thought Denise's feelings toward Leo were as strong as his were for her, but she wouldn't tell him that. She didn't kick a dog when it was down, and this dog was *way* down.

"I have no idea. She told me she was pregnant a few weeks ago."

"You didn't use protection?"

Leo was one of the brightest boys in the school, and he didn't seem like the type who'd lose his head in the heat of the moment.

He grimaced. "Of course we did. I always wore a condom, and she was on the Pill. But she got bronchitis a month or so ago and went on antibiotics. That makes the Pill stop working, which we didn't know. And then," he looked away from her again, "the condom broke one night."

"Is she keeping the baby?"

He nodded. "Said she wanted the baby. Apparently, the only thing she doesn't want is me."

Yvonne couldn't figure out why Denise would choose to raise a baby alone, when the father obviously wanted to marry her and was in love with her. Besides, Leo was great with kids, something she'd witnessed firsthand. Her younger cousins Darcy and Oliver adored Leo. There was no way Denise couldn't believe he would be an awesome father.

"Did she break up with you?" Yvonne asked.

"Yeah."

"What are you going to do?"

Leo shifted on the seat until he was facing her. "That's what I was trying to figure out. I don't know what to do. I can't shirk my responsibility, can't walk away from her, knowing she's having my baby."

Leo was the most upright, honorable guy she'd ever met, if she didn't count the men in her family.

"Who says you have to?"

"What?" he asked.

"The baby is yours too. You have rights. You don't have to be married to her to be a father to your kid. Did you tell your folks?"

He shook his head. "Not yet. They're going to freak the fuck out."

"Yeah." Yvonne's parents would do the same if she ended up in this situation. But she also knew that they would support and help her. "You think they'll kick you out?"

"No. God no. They're not going to be happy, but they'll stand by me. Help me sort it out. I just hate disappointing them. Hate asking..."

He didn't have to finish his sentence. She knew Leo, knew how much he hated asking for help. In a school full of immature, hormone-driven teenage boys, he'd always stood out, always seemed older, always the one who had his shit together.

"They'll help you. It'll work out fine. Neither you nor Denise were planning to go away to college. So you'll work out a schedule. Raise your baby together."

Her plan didn't sound like one he cared for. "That every-other-weekend crap?" He shook his head. "That's a shitty way for a kid to grow up."

"The baby will never know anything different. What's normal for one person isn't normal for the next. As long as you both love the baby and take care of it, it'll be a lucky kid."

Leo fell silent for a long time and for once in her life, she shut up and let him deal with his thoughts. It wasn't that hard to do. She was sort of reeling herself, so she sat there, swimming around in her own head, thinking about how much his life had changed and wondering how she would handle the same circumstance.

Finally, Leo turned to her and smiled. "I'm going to be a good dad."

She grinned back. "You're going to be an *awesome* dad."

Leo looked at her—and for the first time ever, Yvonne got the sense that he really *saw* her, not as part of their group at school, but as a real person on her own. "You're a really good friend, Vonnie. Thanks."

Yvonne smiled wider, despite the tiny pang in her heart that ached at being called just a friend.

YVONNE HAD THOUGHT BACK TO THAT AFTERNOON COUNTLESS times through the years as she'd watched Leo with his son, Vince. Aside from her own dad, Yvonne was certain there wasn't a more devoted, loving father on the planet.

"You know what?" Yvonne said. "I think you're right, Riley. I think I'm going to have to stick my nosy Collins' nose into this and stage an intervention."

Riley wiped her hands on her apron before rubbing them together with glee. There was nothing her aunt liked more than to plot a sneak attack. "Excellent. Here's what I think you should do."

WILD SPIRIT IS AVAILABLE NOW.

ABOUT THE AUTHOR

Virginia native Mari Carr is a New York Times and USA TODAY bestseller of contemporary romance novels. With over two million copies of her books sold, Mari was the winner of the Romance Writers of America's Passionate Plume award for her novella, Erotic Research. She has over a hundred published works, including her popular Wild Irish and Compass books, along with the Trinity Masters series she writes with Lila Dubois.

Follow Mari:
www.maricarr.com
mari@maricarr.com